Cosmopolitan Girls

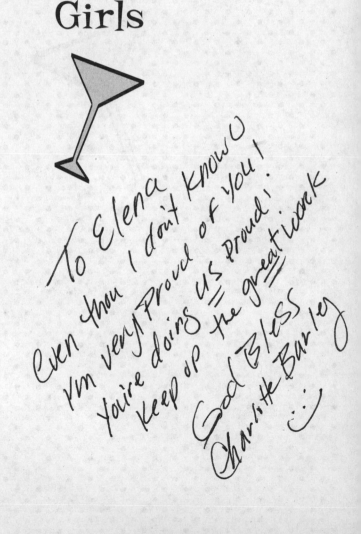

To Elena know ♡
even thou I don't know ♡
I'm very proud of you!
You're doing us proud!
Keep up the great work
God Bless
Charlotte Burley
:)

Cosmopolitan Girls

Charlotte Burley
and
Lyah Beth LeFlore

Harlem Moon • Broadway Books • New York

Published by Harlem Moon, an imprint of Broadway Books, a division of Random House, Inc.

PRINTED IN THE UNITED STATES OF AMERICA

HARLEM MOON, BROADWAY BOOKS, and the HARLEM MOON logo, depicting a moon and a woman, are trademarks of Random House, Inc. The figure in the Harlem Moon logo is inspired by a graphic design by Aaron Douglas (1899–1979).

Visit our website at www.harlemmoon.com

First edition published 2004

Book design by Dana Leigh Treglia

Library of Congress Cataloging-in-Publication Data
Burley, Charlotte.
Cosmopolitan girls / Charlotte Burley & Lyah LeFlore.—1st ed.
p. cm.
1. New York (N.Y.)—Fiction. 2. Female friendship—Fiction. I. LeFlore, Lyah. II. Title.
PS3602.U7S7C67 2004
813'.6—dc21
2003049924

ISBN 0-7679-1567-4

10 9 8 7 6 5 4 3 2 1

Charlotte Burley's Dedication

I give all the Honor, Glory and Praise, to my Lord and Savior, for He has given me this precious gift of creative expression. For without Him it could never be.

Lyah Beth LeFlore's Dedication

To Minnie, Floyd Sr., Annette, and Munro: your spirits live through my work and words.

To my mom, Shirley Bradley LeFlore, my rock, inspiration, and best friend. You held me up when I didn't have the strength to do it on my own. You taught me the importance of prayer and faith, and allowed me to stretch and grow and be all the things I wanted to be. When I make mistakes you hug-me-up and help me start again. When I succeed, you cheer me on from the front line. I *am* because of you!

To my dad, Floyd LeFlore, Jr., for encouraging me to follow my heart and dreams, even when it meant throwing caution to the wind. Always, your Sunflower.

To my sisters, Hope and Jacie, our tears, laughter, joy and pain have given us an unbreakable bond as sisters.

To my niece and nephews, Noelle, Jordan, and Jullian, the reasons I smile. May all your hopes and wishes come true!

To my Aunt Barbara Myers, who's been a continuous source of love, support, and guidance throughout my life. Thank you for helping me to become the woman I am today.

To Alan, my mentor and friend. Thank you for your invaluable support and belief in my dreams.

THE COSMOPOLITAN
1 oz ABSOLUT CITRON   1/2 oz TRIPLE SEC
1/2 oz LIME JUICE   1/2 oz CRANBERRY
JUICE LIME WEDGE SHAKE LIQUID
INGREDIENTS LIKE HELL IN
A SHAKER WITH ICE.
POUR INTO A
CHILLED
MARTINI
GLASS.
GAR-
NISH
WITH A
LIME
TWIST.
"A
drunk
body speaks
a sober mind..."
— Unknown

Part 1

All Is Fair in Love...

Prologue

I'll be the first to admit I was always in love with
the idea of being in love. I used to think, "Oh I
can change him" or "Maybe I'm not being under-
standing enough?" "I should listen more." My favorite was "Hey, if I just hang in there, sooner or
later he'll come around. This man's got potential!" Well to hell with potential. The truth of the
matter is, a woman can't operate on the mights or
maybes, only the what is.

I look back and I realize my mindset was all
wrong. In the midst of always trying to make the
unworkable work out, I lost who I was and almost

lost my sanity. I forgot about my happiness. Sometimes I found myself walking around feeling like I would lose out if I didn't give all I could—sex, time, energy, etc. It didn't help that as I made my daily trek to Starbucks for a grande latte, I saw woman's magazine after woman's magazine that said: "Are we too aggressive?" "Are we giving up the Victoria's Secret too soon?" "Are we too overbearing in our relationships?" "Too Fat?" "Too Skinny?" "Do we love ourselves enough?" It's a wonder we women aren't all crazy from the garbage the media throws at us.

Give us a break y'all!

Been there, done that!

A girl could spend her whole life dodging those pitfalls and warning signs. Instead of putting ourselves through all that hardship, isn't it much simpler to just ask men what they really think? After all, you don't need to give a man *all the goods* if you don't even know what he wants. Does he love you? Does he even like you? Think about it. Friendship is the key to any relationship, male, female, or otherwise, right?

Okay, I'm not some sort of self-proclaimed relationship guru, but my experiences have taught me the hard way, and now I have a much better approach and outlook on life and love. At the end of the day, considering everything that's happened to me, I don't regret a moment. Regret what? I did it! However embarrassing, wonderful, or painful as it was. I had to go through it all to be the woman I am today . . .

Chapter 1

Lindsay Bradley

The invite in fancy gold script read, *Lindsay Bradley you are cordially invited to* Vogue *magazine's after party for the VH1 Fashion Awards at Lotus.* Lotus was one of the hottest clubs in New York City, and reason enough to flex my VP status and slip out of the office by seven. For me, that was like working a half day.

I zipped my candy-apple-red BMW 325I out of the parking garage onto Forty-fourth and Broadway. I called her my "baby," because I'd sacrificed and gone on a serious spending diet to come up with the down payment. Even though I almost died eating frozen dinners for all those months, Baby was my first new car. It felt good to work hard and have something to show for it.

Driving in Manhattan I'd become a master behind the wheel, using quick reflexes to switch in and out of lanes with exact precision and obnoxiously blowing my horn to make the car in front of me get the hell out of the way. This was New York style!

I hit the West Side Highway headed Uptown, pressed power on the radio, and popped the sunroof open, catching a whiff of the Hudson River. Midtown's flashing lights and skyscraping buildings faded into the distance. In no time, I was pulling into the garage across from my building on 122nd.

I lived in a refurbished three-story prewar walk-up. Harlem was the happening place to live. I was a lucky girl! The apartment listing had been hidden in the back of the *Village Voice* so well it almost blended in with the rest of the tiny print, proving you had to be both diligent and desperate to find a great apartment for a decent price in this city.

I heard a loud voice coming toward me. It was Maria, my super Tito's wife. That woman knows she can run her mouth.

"Callate la boca!" Maria screamed down the hallway to Tito, who was still in their apartment.

Too late. *"Ay dios mios!"* she muttered, heading right in my direction. I double-timed it up the steps. I had exactly one hour to transform myself into "fly Lindsay" and be ready to roll with my girls Tara and Judy.

"Hey, *mami?*" Maria said from the bottom of the steps with her hands on her hips.

"Hey Maria!" I called out, narrowly escaping her evening drama.

She was wearing fuzzy flip-flops and a velour two-piece, but had a little too much baby fat for her Baby Phat, if you know what I mean. Her hair was pulled up in a big blond ponytail, perched on top of her head like a bright bird ready to take flight.

" 'Bye Maria!" I called, cutting her off nicely as I closed the door to my apartment.

Once inside, the scent of Illume vanilla and pomegranate candles fragranced the air. I inhaled, exhaled, and pressed play on the stereo. Marvin Gaye's "Got to Give It Up" jump-started the night. My home was like sacred ground to me. My apartment's shabby-chic flair made it both comfortable and practical. On weekends I took full advantage, lounging on the two large down-filled couches in my living room. A small wrought-iron table, surrounded by four chairs draped in ivory slipcovers, sat off to the side. It was obvious, by the thin layer of dust on the glass top, that I rarely dined there. I was especially proud of the black-and-white stills of my grandparents and great-grandparents that adorned the walls.

I checked my answering machine. *Lindsay, you were in my thoughts, be prayerful, be positive, relax, and may God's light of protection surround you.* Mama left another one of her signature inspirational messages—it was just her subtle reminder for me to find a church home. I'd promised myself I'd find one as soon as work eased up. In the meantime, I compromised and purchased a book of daily affirmations.

I undressed and jetted into the hallway, opening the closet that housed my party digs. I pulled out a black Michael Kors dress with a plunging neckline. Yeah, this was the one!

Doing my makeup was always a quick job, applying a good moisturizer, lip gloss, and brow powder. Simple was safe, same with the hair—long hair was my trademark and I kept a low-maintenance blunt cut. Finally, I was ready to complete my transformation into "fly Lindsay." I quickly abandoned the small diamond studs and classic stainless steel Rolex that marked my "professional" look, and pulled out a pair of large rhinestone hoops and a matching choker.

Tara and Judy pulled up right on time.

"Lin Lin!" Tara exclaimed in a high-pitched nasally voice. I hated the nickname she started using out of the blue. But I loved her too much to tell her to stop.

"I like! I like!" I said, checking out her new XJ5. It still smelled fresh off the assembly line.

Tara was wearing her usual midriff. I'd kill for her abs! When she hit thirty, two years ago, she became a fitness fanatic, and now she never misses an opportunity to show some skin.

"On time for a change!" Judy started blabbering away as usual. If you looked up *drama* in the dictionary a picture of Judy would be there. Judy truly believed that a person had no excuse to be unattractive. Hair extensions, breast implants, and tummy tucks weren't just for the famous, and she had experimented with them all. The one thing she left unchanged was her face. Judy was a natural cutie.

Tara is an ad exec at a big firm, and Judy's a publicist for many of the popular hip-hop artists. They're both East Coast born and bred and I'm a Midwesterner, but living in New York for the past five years, I've almost earned my honorary New Yorker status.

The line in front of Lotus was halfway down the block, but the doorman knew us and ushered us quickly past the infamous velvet rope. Inside, A-list celebrities paraded before us: Pink, Justin Timberlake, Madonna, and Robert De Niro. We went straight to the bar that ran the length of the narrow club and ordered a round of Cosmopolitans.

"We'll have three Cosmos, and *please*, no house vodka. Absolut Citron, light on the cranberry and lime juice," I said, giving a friendly wink to the female bartender, who looked fresh off a Paris runway.

"You'll have to excuse her, she thinks she's some kind of Cosmo connoisseur," Judy shouted over the music.

"I like the sound of that! See, I just know the difference between a so-so Cosmopolitan and a great one, and I *only* drink great ones."

The bartender shook the cocktail shaker to the beat of an infectious bass line, then gingerly poured a frothy pink liquid into three chilled martini glasses.

"See if this suits your palate," the bartender said, winking back at me.

"Perfecto!" I said, giving her my approval. "You got skills, and I *will* be back."

I gave the bartender a high-five as Judy, Tara, and I

grabbed our drinks and moved past partygoers dressed in the latest haute couture. Some people just stood bobbing their heads, others posed on low ottomans like they were in a *Vogue* layout.

We pushed our way into the narrow, overcrowded VIP area, behind yet another velvet rope. I immediately noticed a pair of eyes I'd seen once before. They were greenish-gray and hypnotic.

"Lindsay? Whassup? It's Troy. We met a while ago through my boy Randy Lanier," he said, helping me into a booth, trying his best to talk over the bass.

"Oh right! I think I remember. It's good to see you again."

Despite my reply, I knew *exactly* who he was and remembered every detail of the night I met him: Randy's birthday dinner at Jezebel and we flirted with each other all night. I even remember what he had on: a black turtleneck, black slacks, and a Cartier Tank watch. Just what I liked, simple, stylish, classy, and chivalrous—he even helped me with my coat at the end of the night. I was sure I'd never see him again since he lived in the Bay Area. What was Troy doing in New York now?

Suddenly, out of nowhere, Judy burst in between us grabbing me by the arm.

I was out of breath when we finally stopped in front of the ladies' room. "Forget that man. I'm trying to get us to the powder room. Tara and I have a surprise!" Judy said. I was pissed, this better be good. "What hot actress have you been talking about starring in your new series?" she asked. There was only one person she could be talking about. Alix

Alexander. Latest Bond chick, and soon-to-be costar in Will Smith's new movie. I was dying to work with her.

We walked into the cramped bathroom. The ladies' room was a subculture in and of itself. Even though we go there to "freshen up," we made sure we did a once-over adjustment to look good before going in. It's all about making an entrance.

The room was buzzing with women searching for everything from hairbrushes to breath mints. Tara was already inside at the mirror putting on lipstick. Another woman, standing next to her, turned around. It was Alix. She was giving me major attitude, looking me up and down.

"Alix, this is our girl Lindsay," Tara said, signaling I was cool.

"Hey, Lindsay. It's really good to meet you." Alix's look quickly went from cold to warm. I had to give her her props. She could dress her ass off and her hair was always slammin'. I joined them at the mirror, opened my purse, and began rummaging through it, looking for my Mac lip glass. The other women were hanging around and checking us out. I could hear the whispers and feel the catty looks.

As I applied my lip liner and lip glass, from the corner of my eye I noticed we were the topic of a trio's conversation.

"Isn't that Alix Alexander?" the short one asked, popping her gum.

"Yep, but she ain't that pretty in person," her friend added, in a nasally voice.

"I heard she's sleeping with Vin Diesel *and* 50 Cent!" the tallest one said, out the side of her mouth.

I turned toward them. The tallest one knew I had heard their entire conversation. "Ooh, girl, you are working those shoes." She pointed to my feet, giving me a phony smile.

"Thanks," I returned, equally artificial, as the women quickly walked out the door.

In the mirror's reflection I saw a woman trying to calm down her girlfriend who was crying hysterically. Her eye makeup had smeared like melted licorice all over her face, and her hair looked like a powder puff.

"Oh my God, can you believe he came with her? I'm gonna fuck both of them up! How does my hair look?"

"It looks great!" her friend said, patting the woman's hair unsuccessfully before giving up and walking over to the sink.

"Excuse me," she said, stepping between Alix and me, taking a paper towel and wetting it, and returning to the weeping friend. "You can't let him see you like this," she said, giving her a pep talk as they exited.

A tipsy woman, doing a nail-biting balancing act in three-inch heels, was near the door arguing with the West Indian bathroom attendant after trying to skip out on a tip.

"All I got was a paper towel and a spritz of perfume."

"You got four sticks of gum, too."

"Urgh!" she said, tossing two dollars into the tip basket and teetering out the door.

Suddenly, everyone's attention shifted to a woman whose weak stomach was proof she'd had too much to drink. She rushed into a nearby stall and spent the next several minutes communing with the porcelain god.

Just then another woman who I didn't recognize entered and joined us. She and Alix hugged.

"This is my girl Camille, everybody," Alix said. Camille looked like a waif model without the height. Before we could get the cordials out, Alix called, "That's the jam!" Hearing the funky beat from the next room, Camille headed for the door, reaching for Alix's hand. Alix grabbed my hand, and without saying a word, we all stepped out of the ladies' room, dancing and bobbing our heads to the music.

Chapter 2

Charlie Thornton

Have you ever felt disappointed, frustrated, confused, and just downright disgusted with yourself? To the point that all you want to do is just lay down and cry? Well that's exactly what I'm doing right now. I mean I'm crying like a big baby. Snotty nose, red puffy eyes, and enough Kleenex to bury myself in sorrow. An act I'm fully capable of committing at this stage. If you must know, I'm having my very own private pity party. A pity party of one. That's because I, Charlie Thornton, am one pitiful child. Only,

I'm not a child. Thirty-two years old is far from juvenile, but my behavior at this moment would have you think otherwise.

Let me help you understand my pain. It's three in the morning and I'm sitting in the middle of a complete mess . . . my life. I've been sitting in front of my computer staring at the same Act 4, Scene 1 . . . for about five years now. No I'm not having writer's block, because that would require me to actually be a writer. Which I'm sad to report, for the last four years, I haven't been. "Miss Charlie Thornton, the famous and talented writer who took New York City by storm": that was supposed to be the cover story. Front page of the *Buffalo Challenger*. The local black news publication in my hometown.

How stupid do I look? I left my hometown five years ago, bragging to my family and friends that I was moving to the big city to make it. Put Buffalo on the map like Rick James did back in the day. I had a foolproof plan: in five years I was going to have my first screenplay on the big screen in theaters all across America. Instead the same "screenplay" is only on a seventeen-inch computer monitor, playing in the private theater of my Brooklyn basement apartment.

You want to know the sad part, I have no one to blame. Losing focus and getting sidetracked from my master plan was all my own doing. No one forced me to say yes. No one forced me to toss my goals to the side and put other people's happiness first. Nope, that was my choice. That's why I just need to shut the hell up, quit my whining, and take my loser ass to bed, so that I can get up in the morning and face reality.

Are you sure you want to shut down? my computer just flashed, asking me the ultimate question of the night.

"Ah, ya think!" I said sarcastically, as I pressed enter and dragged my sorry tail to bed.

Chapter 3

You Go Girl

The party was in full swing, and I was standing on my chair shaking everything and more that my mama had given me to the hot sounds DJ Biz Markie was pumping. Alix was getting her groove on too, dancing with Camille on top of the table like a wild woman.

Judy and Tara were blissfully sandwiched between two exotic male model hotties. I took a break from dancing with Alix and Camille. They were definitely professional club rats. I was high, but when I looked at my watch and saw it was

2 A.M., I knew it was time to go home. I had to be at work by seven. Even in party mode I knew when to shut it down.

Bright and early I'm on the grind again. When I step through that big glass revolving door into MediaMax's massive lobby, this is my world and I put my game face on.

Right now it's all about playing my cards right, and I'm trying to break through all kinds of glass ceilings. I'm busting my butt daily to reach my five-year goal: make a move from VP into a fat in-house producer's deal, then come back into the fold as a full-time suit, becoming the first black female president of a network.

This morning I sat across from my boss listening intently to his words.

"Lindsay, let's make sure your key focus for the next thirty days is putting together the best Upfront MediaMax has ever had." My boss Robert Gatewood's coarse but energetic words would be etched into my brain and I would eat, sleep, and live them for the next month.

"It's all about the advertising dollars."

The Upfront was an annual presentation event where the cable and major networks set out to prove to advertisers that their dollars were well spent. The networks also went head-to-head, dazzling the advertisers with the best presentation of what each had to offer.

MediaMax was one of the biggest media conglomerates, up there with Time Warner and Viacom. MediaMax owns several magazines, New York's number-one radio station, and four cable networks, no, make that five. Exhale, Lifetime's new competition, was our latest acquisition.

This was Robert's first Upfront since becoming CEO. He oversaw the five cable networks. Little did he know I didn't need thirty days; I was already prepared with a slew of ideas.

"What's our theme?" Robert drilled.

"This year's Upfront is about nostalgia and strong brand identity."

I could feel Robert dissecting my ideas before I got them out.

"On the Style Channel, consider our new pilot *Flip Moda*, where classic designers go head-to-head with hot new designers, perfect pitch for Coca-Cola Classic. For the Video Music Network and Hit Music TV channels, we'll feature a cross-generation of music specials like *Divas Doin' It* and *Hiphopera*. It'll be great for Ford and their business."

Eat that!

"Okay, you've given me enough for now, some interesting ideas. I like the direction you're headed in," he replied coolly.

"Robert, one more quick thing. I also think we should think about a hot female-driven drama series. It would be a great lead-off for Exhale, since the channel doesn't have any original programming yet," I said.

"Lindsay, not so fast. You're getting ahead of yourself. This Upfront I want to concentrate on what we have. Exhale is a future creative discussion. In the meantime, you're onto something with the other stuff, but you need to dig deeper.

"I want you to come back tomorrow morning with some

stronger thoughts and a bigger idea list. Remember, thirty days to put together a helluva schedule that will bury the competition and score some major advertising."

My confidence had taken a blow, but now was not the time to pout. Sure, Robert put the pressure on me, but I was his protégé. The only female on his executive team, and I was definitely going places. Robert was going to make sure of that . . . and so was I.

I was fueled, so I decided to keep working through lunch. Unfortunately, my hunger pangs wouldn't let me. I figured I'd compromise and grab some quick brain food from the lobby café and come back to my desk. With Robert on my back I had my work cut out for me. My phone rang.

"Lindsay Bradley."

"How's my busy daughter?" Mama asked.

"I'm good. How you doing, Mama?" I'd forgotten about the mental note I'd made to call her. "I'm sorry, but I'm really swamped. I can't talk long."

"You know I hate to call you at work, but I just wanted to remind you to give your sister a call."

"Which one?" I said. I had two sisters, and it was hard keeping up on everybody's lives.

"Lindsay! I can't believe you. Your sister Faith! That MRI's tomorrow and I want you to keep her in your prayers."

"That's right!" I felt awful. How could I forget? "Let me run so I can call her before my next meeting. I gotta go! Love you!"

"I love you too. And slow down, Lindsay. I worry about you. Say your prayers," Mama said, concerned. "And call Angie too, she said she hasn't heard from you in a week."

I stopped what I was doing and quickly dialed Faith. Faith's test was critical since the doctor suspected she had MS. Faith had gone through a series of tests, but this was the big one.

"Hello?" Faith answered, sounding like she was out of breath.

"Hey girl, it's me, Lindsay. You must be fooling with those kids." Faith was a homemaker who spent her afternoons planning Jack-and-Jill socials, and picking out new wallpaper. "I want you to know I'm praying that all goes well with your test tomorrow."

"I thought I wasn't gonna hear from you," Faith said, making sure I felt guilty.

"You know I couldn't forget about my big sis," I said, grabbing my wallet and checking the time. "Ugh! Faith I'm sorry, but my day is crazy."

"Don't sweat it. Get off the phone, don't work too hard, and call me later."

"I won't and I will. I love you. Don't worry, the test will be fine. I'll check on you after," I said and hung up. I closed my eyes and said a quick but powerful prayer.

I hopped on the elevator just as the doors were closing and occupied myself by reading over my ideas on the ride down. The doors opened and I stepped out still lost in thought.

"We have to stop meeting like this."

I didn't have to turn around. I knew that voice anywhere. A smile spread across my face. "So, what, are you following me now?" I said, turning to find myself trapped in Troy's gaze yet again. The second time in less than twenty-four hours. This time I wouldn't let this man get away.

"I've got a meeting on twenty-five at Video Music Network, but before I lose you again, can I please get your number?" Troy asked with raised eyebrow.

I could see he wasn't taking any chances either. We didn't waste another second swapping business cards.

"I have to go out of the country to shoot a Jennifer Lopez video, but I'll be back in two weeks. When I get back can we get together for dinner?" he asked, as he looked half at my card and half at me.

I was trying my best not to get carried away. He was too cute, in an overgrown boyish kind of way, and the more I looked at him, the more I blushed.

"So?" he asked again.

I was still smiling. "In two weeks? Hmmm, that would be nice . . . really nice."

Chapter 4

Superwoman

Before I knew it 6 A.M. had rolled around and now I was mad that I had stayed up so late feeling sorry for myself.

"I can't find my shoes!" yelped Tiffany, the youngest crewmember of what I called Company B. *B* stood for *baby*.

"Tiffany did you look underneath the bed?" I yelled, continuing to set the breakfast table.

"Oh yeah, I found them," Tiffany said, running her tiny six-year-old body to the table. Hair so wild, only baby oil and a stern brush could help me tame it. But my ritual of combing it after she ate always allowed me a few extra minutes to get a kick out of just how cute she is. I leaned over, kissed her cheek, and slid a plate of hotcakes in front of her.

My biggest baby of them all, Michael, a.k.a. my better half, frantically searched the apartment for his work boots.

"Michael your work boots are in the laundry room," I said while I pointed. I suddenly remembered that I had left his shirt on the ironing board. I wasn't quite sure if I'd ironed it, but when Michael joined us in the kitchen wrinkle-free, I remembered that I had completed that task just before I finished pressing Michael Junior's pants.

Michael gave me my morning kiss before taking his seat next to Tiffany.

"MJ!" I called. "Is he still in that bathroom? I bet he's trying to see if he has a mustache," I joked, questioning the whereabouts of baby number three. "MJ get out here before your food gets cold," I called out again.

As he came into the kitchen I pecked MJ on his cheek and waited for him to wipe it off, as if it were bug repellent. I was surprised when he just sat down and started to eat.

"No wiping my kiss today?" I said, sitting down.

"Naw, not today. I guess I'll let you slide," MJ said, looking up at me with the same big brown eyes and jet-black curly hair his father has. That boy is the spitting image of Michael, and at eight years old, he's already a trip.

Michael and MJ were headed out the door when suddenly Michael turned back.

"Charlie, don't kill me. I know this is last minute, but after you pick up Tiffany from day care, I need you to pick up MJ too." He tried to give me a sad face. "Please babe? I

totally forgot that I have to work a double shift tonight."
Michael knew that what he was asking wasn't fair. Tiffany's
day-care center was closer to the house, but MJ's day camp
was on the East Side of Manhattan, nowhere near my job.
"I promise I'll make it up to you. Next weekend I'll pam-
per you just how you like it." Michael always knew how to
soften me up.

Picking up Tiffany *and* MJ was a big favor, but Michael
always keeps his promises. That's one of the things I love
about him. So, knowing him like I do, I would come out on
the better end of the deal later.

"Okay, but you owe me," I smiled back.

"Five-thirty," MJ blurted out.

"Boy, I know!" I laughed, closing the door only to turn
around to see Tiffany standing in the middle of the hallway
with a broken rubber band in hand and a huge portion of
hair sticking straight up.

"I didn't do it," she said, shrugging her shoulders.

After what already felt like a full day of work, miraculously,
I made it to my "real job" on time. I briskly walked across
Rockefeller Center and entered the side door to my office
building. When I stepped off the elevator onto the third
floor, the first face I saw was Kyle's, a dead ringer for Bryant
Gumbel. He was an old college buddy, and I'm sad to say
my only friend other than Michael in the entire city of
New York.

"Kyle!" I said, greeting him with a warm hug.

"My girl! So, I hear congratulations are in order."

"What are you talking about?" I said as we made our
way to my office.

"Don't tell me you haven't heard. Everyone is talking about your ad campaign, and how it served as the key tool for Miranda to seal the deal with B-Caps!" Kyle said.

Miranda was the vice president of Imagination City, the advertising agency I write copy for. Thanks to Kyle, a freelance consultant for the company, who rescued me from temping. Temp agencies often found it difficult to place me, with my natural unprocessed hair and throwback seventies style. If you know what I mean.

"Really? So everyone is talking?" I gave a slight grin.

"Yes, sounds to me like somebody's due for a bonus check," Kyle said, grabbing a seat, pulling it up to my desk.

"From your mouth to God's ear. A bonus would be perfect right now," I said, hopeful, glancing at the photos of Michael and the kids that adorned my desktop.

"Why, so you can buy more of these *expensive* posters? I see there's a new edition," Kyle said, looking around my modest office, pointing to one from the hit series *Soul Food*. "Whoa, and honey I can understand why! If them ain't some fine brothers in that show!" said Kyle, who was openly gay.

"That's not the reason I got that poster, thank you very much," I said, laughing.

Collecting black movie posters was a hobby I'd developed after seeing the film *The Best Man*. I was so proud when I saw it—not once but three times—that I went on a shopping spree and purchased the poster. I made a promise to myself that every couple of months I'd splurge on a new poster from the new breed of black filmmakers. So far I have the soon-to-be classics *Boyz N the Hood, Menace to*

Society, and the original *Soul Food* movie, as well as the TV series poster. That last one was an exception, like Kyle said—those brothers are too fine! Next quest, *Brown Sugar*, and hopefully, one day soon, a Charlie Thornton.

Susan, another copywriter, poked her head in the door.

"Charlie, congratulations on your *little* spot," she said with a smile that felt more like a warning than an actual compliment. "Kyle, I didn't see you in there," she winked, and then said, "Oh well, gotta run, I'm working on something big for Miranda."

As soon as Susan was out of sight, Kyle closed the door, placing his hand on his hips.

"Now that heifer knows damn well she saw me!"

"Kyle! I'm having a positive day so let's just try to keep it that way."

"Well, all I know, Miss Honey, is that you better watch *Blond Ambition*. She is not your friend. And these people better recognize the fact that you da bomb, okay!" Kyle said, emphatically.

I cracked a smile knowing all too well that he was speaking the truth.

Huffing and puffing I found myself out of breath running toward MJ's day camp. I was a half hour late, thanks to yet another track fire on the subway. MJ's long face and silence vilified my tardiness even more.

"MJ baby, I'm so sorry I'm late but there was a fire on the train—"

"Whatever!" MJ interrupted my plea.

"How about I make it up to you and treat you and

Tiffany to some ice cream at Ben & Jerry's?" I said, trying to win him over.

"Listen Charlie, stop trying to act like you're my mama. You ain't, okay!" He rolled his eyes, "Man I can't wait to get back to my mama's house!" MJ smarted off as he b-boy strutted away.

Chapter 5

Prince Charming

I kept watching the clock all day like a school-kid. Troy called two weeks to the day and our first date is tonight. Unfortunately, Robert and I were deep in a brainstorming session for the Upfront. I two-wayed Troy, letting him know I was running late, and I'd meet him at the restaurant. Troy insisted on picking me up at the office.

I was uncomfortable with him doing that so soon. I wasn't ready for Robert to be privy to my private life. Robert hired me and took me under his wing five years ago, and from day one he stressed that one should avoid excessive socializing. A person would have more than enough time to enjoy all that on the other side of success. As far as Robert was concerned I lived for MediaMax. I was his faithful, trusted right hand. Therefore, I never mixed the business Lindsay with the social Lindsay, and that was that.

This particular night Robert and I were working after hours, and everyone else had gone home. Before leaving, Robert's assistant posted our Upfront plans on large boards in Robert's office where there was more space and privacy. When Robert started running the company, he implemented what he called an open-door policy. All the executives were in cubicles. He felt it would boost company morale to have the entire staff mixing and mingling.

Robert's office was on a whole different level. It was as meticulous as he was. In the center of the room sat a massive mahogany desk, sparsely decorated with matching leather accessories, surrounded by large windows. A butter-soft imported leather sofa that sat across from it was the only other ostentatious object in the room. A small halogen bulb spotlighted the glass shelves of his bookcase where rows of Emmys, Aces, and certificates of achievement were prominently displayed.

We had just about wrapped up for the night and for the thousandth time, I checked my watch. Nine o'clock. Troy said he'd be here between nine and nine-fifteen. I was standing in front of the biggest picture window behind Robert's desk when he returned from the bathroom. The skyline and city below looked so much better from inside his gigantic piece of the world. Robert quietly leaned over my shoulder.

"I think we've done some good work tonight. You really came up with some exciting ideas, Lindsay."

"I guess taking another stab at it wasn't so bad," I said, smiling, looking up at him.

I'd been wondering the whole night about the position of Robert's large leather swivel desk chair. "Robert, why does your chair always face toward the window?" I asked curiously.

Robert paused, taking a deep breath. "I like to look out onto the world and think about things like life and where I want to be at fifty. It helps me clear my head and strategize what I'll conquer next," he said with the look of a warrior in his eyes.

Robert was a deep brother, and for the first time I really looked at him. His skin was dark like a melted Hershey bar, keen features, clean-shaven, and he kept a low haircut. His soft shiny waves gave away that he used an expensive ethnic pomade to keep the tiny strands in place. Robert was lean, six feet, and forty-two. Younger than one would imagine, since he was so powerful in the industry.

"So you plan to conquer it alone? No wife, no kids?" My words had slipped out before I could stop them. Maybe I'd gotten too comfortable? Robert paused again. I got nervous. He turned to me and spoke softly. "Lindsay, relationships distract people from their goals. I guess that's the very reason I've stayed single."

His words lingered, and so did his eye contact. It seemed that there was a connection a bit deeper than Media-Max . . .

"Excuse me?" Troy said, poking his head in Robert's office, "Am I interrupting something?"

I was as startled as if he'd just caught me in the arms of another man. Robert's attitude was just the opposite.

"Can I help you?" he said with an air of arrogance.

"Uh, no, Robert, this is my friend Troy," I said, fumbling, walking toward Troy. I wanted to hug him, but then I'd be really putting my business out there. Why was I tripping so hard? I had waited all this time to see Troy and now I didn't even want to greet him properly. Get it together girl!

Before I could make any introductions, Troy had stepped into Robert's office and was extending his hand.

"Hello, I'm Troy Barnes," he said, offering a firm handshake.

"Good meeting you," Robert said, shaking Troy's hand like he was sizing him up. He didn't even bother to give Troy his name. Robert then turned to me. He was so good he could dismiss you without you even knowing it, but I knew. He was flat-out dissing Troy.

"Lindsay, I think we're done. I'll see you bright and early tomorrow."

"Thanks Robert," I said, ushering Troy out as fast as I could. Robert's stiff body language told me not to even think about getting my groove on too hard tonight. Why was Robert coming off possessive?

I could breathe now, and was glad Troy and Robert's pissing war was over. The night had started off rocky, but Troy seemed determined to make every aspect of our first date perfect. I loved Italian food and the SoHo restaurant Barolo was one of my favorites. It was elegant, airy, and had a beautiful garden.

Troy and I had been talking for what seemed like hours, just gazing into each other's eyes. I had a crazy spiritual thing about eyes. Mama said they were the windows to a person's soul.

"What's up with the dude at your job? He's kinda cocky. I don't dig that," Troy said, pouring me another glass of Merlot.

I was hoping we could just let that slide. I should've known better. "No, my boss Robert's cool. He's just a little intense," I said, slightly defensive.

"I just didn't know if I was breaking something up or not." Troy was giving me shit on the sly.

"Troy, you don't have anything to worry about," I said, reaching over and gently touching his hand. Troy smiled, taking the subtle hint to let it go. "So, tell me about yourself, Troy."

"What do you want to know?" he replied.

"Everything!"

"Okay. You may or may not know, I'm a video director, a Virgo, a Morehouse man, of course, and the youngest of three boys. Well, I was," he said, clearing his throat. "A brotha didn't mean to get all emotional on the first date, but my oldest brother died three years ago in a car accident."

We sat silently and awkwardly for a few minutes.

"I'm sorry to hear that. I'm the baby of three girls, and I don't know what I'd do if I lost one of my sisters. It must really be hard to deal with."

"Yeah, it still gets rough sometimes. He was more like a father to me, because our father wasn't around. He taught me everything," he said, this time taking a sip of his wine.

"I feel you. There's a good chance my oldest sister has MS. The doctors are still running a bunch of tests, but I'm praying she doesn't have it."

"I'll say a prayer too."

"Thanks. A sista didn't mean to get all emotional on the first date, either."

We both laughed.

I was starting to dig this guy already. I had to get straight to the point. "So, Troy, is there a lady in your life?"

"C'mon, give a brotha some credit. If I had a woman I wouldn't be here with you."

"Okay, I'll give you that. So when you do have a woman, what kind of things do you like to do?"

"I like to do it all, picnics, horseback riding, anything outdoors. I love to travel, shop, and spontaneity is my middle name."

I started to blush. Why did I suddenly feel like I was on *The Dating Game*?

"Look, Lindsay, I don't want to play games with you. I'm looking to get to know you, get in your head, see what Lindsay's all about. I'm feelin' you," Troy said, looking me in the eye.

I had never heard a man speak his intentions up front before. It let me know it was okay for me to be direct too.

"You know that I dated your boy Randy?" I kept strong eye contact and didn't blink.

"Are you with him now?"

"No, but it didn't end well."

"Lindsay, I'm a grown man and you're a grown woman and neither one of us is married. The past is the past. He's my boy, but he don't run me!"

I've been waiting and wishing for an honest and solid relationship ever since I moved to New York. Men have a tendency to get amnesia when it comes to telling the truth, or get flaky when it comes to sticking with plans. After tonight, though, I think we could really be onto something new, exciting and meaningful.

Troy is different from the other men I've been dating, with their polished-prep-boy looks and tight bodies. Troy is manly in his six-one build, and I'm champagne and cashmere mixed with some down-home girl-next-door to his Jimi Hendrix "Purple Haze" and Abercrombie & Fitch. Troy is definitely in his own category. His goatee and the big sandy curls that make up his low-fro are an extension of his artistic side.

I'm captivated by his intelligence, too. This man knows about everything from stocks and bonds to world events. Damn, a brother with a good head on his shoulders, *husband* material. Without a doubt.

Chapter 6

Surprise!

Believe it or not but picking up that brat MJ from day camp last week turned out to be worth it. Don't get me wrong, it's not easy being in my position. I have really grown to love that boy as if he were my own, but as MJ and his mother, Juanita, like to remind me, those are not my kids. It's strange, but I didn't start hearing that until after Michael moved in with me two years ago. I guess like most "baby mamas," Juanita was hoping she and Michael would get back together one day. I don't blame MJ. Like most kids he just wants his parents to be together and live in the same house. So I guess the constant "baby mama drama" I experience is in a way justified.

I knew what I was getting myself into when I met Michael. Accepting him and his baggage, including his every-other-weekend-with-the-kids arrangement. After falling in love with him three years ago, this was a price I was willing to pay. Damn, love is strong sometimes.

But like I said, Michael does keep his promises. So what I thought was going to be a typical trip to the grocery store turned into an overnight stay in the Poconos. He found the cutest little bed-and-breakfast online. Gotta love that Internet!

The innkeeper was an older Irish woman, in her late fifties, whose family had owned the property since the thirties. The soft bags under her eyes gave her a striking resemblance to a cocker spaniel. She tended to our every need, from personally showing us to our room to giving us a tour of the quaint town.

"You like the room?" Michael proudly asked as he began to unpack what appeared to be more surprises from an overnight bag. I nodded yes as I made my way over to see. He pulled out a sexy black lace teddy and let it dangle from his fingers. That was my cue. I sexily catwalked over to him, looking up coyly, like a true innocent. This was all part of our game and, ironically, part of our sexual history.

Growing up in a strict church-going family, sex was for marriage only. I wasn't a virgin when I met Michael but I wasn't far from it. Michael threw me onto the bed and yanked my jeans off. "You ready for the tootsie roll," he said, kissing my navel, making his way down to what he calls my tootsie. Then he began rolling that wicked tongue. Bashful, I tried to cover my excitement.

Oral sex was still very taboo to me. Michael pushed my hands away from my face and held them down firmly. "Baby, look at your man when he's working," his sexy baritone voice commanded, sending chills up my body. Michael may just be the most romantic man I've ever been with, and the freakiest as well . . .

After an erotic shower with Michael, I finally slipped into the teddy and crawled into bed, lying on top of him. "Oh yeah, I forgot to give you this," Michael said, pulling a little box from underneath the pillow. A beautiful tennis bracelet was inside and I didn't know what to say.

I find myself being outdone by him all the time. I remember our first date. I was fifteen minutes late, so I arrived with a dozen red roses in hand. I thought I was really doing something. Michael said he'd never gotten flowers before and was impressed.

For our second date, before he picked me up, about twelve dozen long-stem white roses showed up at my job. I was so undone as the delivery guy crammed all those vases into my tiny office, and so was everyone else who was watching. Humph, I think I'm still blushing from that day. Falling in love with him was easy. Michael may have a lot of baggage, but his knack for romance gets me every time.

Relaxed and tension-free, Michael and I were pulling up into the driveway.

"Home sweet home," I said, following our marvelous weekend away, but I wished we could have stayed up in the

Poconos forever. Michael laughed as he opened the car door to let me out.

"I promise to take you away more often. Okay?" Michael said with a loving look.

The telephone was ringing as we entered the apartment. I picked up, noticing our answering machine had been quite busy while we were away.

"Hello?" I said, wondering who the twenty messages were from. It was strange that the same number appeared several times on the screen. Probably one of those computerized solicitors selling something I didn't need. I jotted down the number on my mini postboard, in case it was important. It was my granny on the other end.

"Hey, Granny."

"Hey!" she chuckled like she always did when she heard my voice. I loved that about her. No matter how good or bad I felt, I could always count on her to lift my spirits.

"Where has my grandbaby been? I've been calling since yesterday and all morning today." Granny loved to fuss. "That message you left me about MJ had me worried. My grand sounding like she losing her mind down there. Chile, you better talk to me," Granny demanded.

"Everything is better now. Michael treated me to an overnight getaway. Actually we were just walking through the door," I said, trying to reassure her that I was fine.

"That's what I like to hear. Now as for that little MJ, his butt just needs a good beating!" Granny and I both giggled.

"I know that's right, but I'll leave that up to Michael," I said, lowering my voice.

"Why are you whispering? Is Michael nearby?"

"Well sort of. You know how small this apartment is. I'll

call you tomorrow from the office and tell you all about MJ's little tantrum," I said.

"Okay, don't forget. Oh, and before *I* forget, I wanted to let you know that I spoke to the caterer today. Your Jewish friends will be happy to know there will be no problem providing a few kosher dishes for the wedding," my granny said, and all I could do was release a sigh of relief.

"What would I do without you!"

"Lord knows I'm going to do everything in my power to make sure Buffalo sees the most extravagant wedding this city has ever seen!"

Ever since my engagement was announced, Granny's been like the wedding police. And my mother, Joyce, her main deputy.

Okay, so now you know. Michael and I are living in sin. We are not married, but we're on our way. Michael proposed to me a year ago and I immediately hollered yes! I mean isn't "Will you marry me?" the question we women wait most of our lives for? The question that drives most of us to the gym, to the beauty salons, and even sometimes to the plastic surgeon. Doing whatever it takes to make sure we're at our best, hoping to trap a man and get him to say "Will you be my wife?"

Well, that's exactly what Michael said to me before placing a hell of a ring on my finger. I'm still coming to grips with Michael having children from a previous relationship. It's overwhelming at times. But the kids aren't that bad. Like I said, some sacrifices are worth it . . . right?

Chapter 7

Caught Up

I stood proudly next to Robert center stage at Radio City Music Hall. I was running on fumes and pure adrenaline, but we did it! Our presentation was solid, and as the theater emptied out, I soaked it all in for the last time and shifted my focus to Robert, who was finishing up an interview with *Entertainment Weekly*. No better time than right now.

"Robert, I took to heart our conversation the other day, and I agree in order to make a splash on Exhale it's gonna take a star. What would you say if I could deliver Alix Alexander?" I said, walking alongside him as we talked.

"I'd say fantastic. But it'll never happen in a million years. She's too hot right now. Alix is a huge movie star."

"I know her and she's psyched about doing a one-hour show about a female cop who is tormented by her past. All I need to know is if I get her in a room with you and a hot writer, can we do this?" I wasn't backing down.

"You are *persistent*, Lindsay Bradley," Robert said, shaking his head and walking away. I was sure he'd left me hanging, until he turned back around midstride. "But I like it. You pull it together and I'll guarantee a pilot, maybe even some episodes."

"That's all I needed to hear." I was ready to make my move.

I told Robert when I first took this job that one of my dreams was to produce for television. So, I plan on taking some serious time and putting the elements of this show together: the star, the writer—and then I'll convince him that I can produce it.

I coasted through the Upfront and Robert was getting praised by the media and the chairman as if he were the prodigal son who had saved the company. Robert made sure my contributions weren't overlooked. I got a nice mention in daily *Variety* and the awkward moment exchanged that night in his office was never mentioned again. Robert respects me and he's proving that he really wants me to succeed. I know he wouldn't do anything to cross that line and jeopardize everything he's built.

I got Robert excited about the idea of going after a big star to do a drama series for Exhale. I would produce it and Alix would star. Alix and I had developed a great rapport.

We hung out a few more times before she headed back to L.A. to start shooting her new movie. She loved the show idea too. Alix liked to party and have a good time, and I perfected the art of schmoozing, courtesy of my corporate American Express card.

"Lin Lin!" Tara waved me over to the booth where she and Judy were on what looked to be their second round.

"Hey, here's to the girl who's the toast of the town. Nice mention in the trades," Judy said, handing me a fresh Cosmopolitan, as I sat down.

"What's the 411, ladies?" Judge Judy ordered. Court was in session.

"The 411 is, I got a man! I'm crazy about some Troy y'all. He treats me good and we have so much fun when we're together. None of that big-dog, shot-caller crap, treating me like I'm an accessory in his life. We talk, vibe, and Troy makes love to my mind." I was caught up!

"All that's fab, but what about the sex!" Judy exclaimed.

"No sex," I said, sipping my drink.

"Excuse me?" Judy interjected, clearing her throat.

"Hold up! Lin Lin. You mean to tell us you haven't let go of the good stuff yet?" Tara was shocked.

"Nope! This time I wanted things to be different. Maybe have a chance at a lasting relationship. It's hard 'cause you know I'm a firm believer in giving it up on the first date," I said, as we all broke into naughty laughter.

"Damn! What's it been, a month?" Tara rolled her eyes. "But, I hear you. I need that kind of self-control."

"I'm not mad at you either," Judy interjected. "All I

know is he's the complete package we all want and strive for, the 'Ultimate Prize.' This man could give a girl everything she ever wanted: marriage, seven figures, a palatial estate in Closter, New Jersey, babies, and serious shopping in Barneys' procreation department," she said longingly.

"Hello!" I added, giving Tara and Judy a soul-sista high five.

Not that Judy had to tell me. I knew Troy was a rising star. He was one of the top video directors in the industry and soon he would be a paid *high* seven-figga-jigga!

And here comes my man now . . .

Troy was walking through the door headed straight for our table.

"Hey Troy," Tara said, scooting over to make room as he bent over to kiss me.

"Whassup Tara? Whassup up Judy?" Troy politely greeted.

"Hey T!" Judy greeted, giving her famous air smooches. "By the way, that new Busta video is the bomb!"

"That's 'cause my man is the bomb!" I said, sexily putting my arm around him.

My cell rang. I cringed. "I'm sorry, I thought I turned it off." I fumbled for the phone.

"Robert didn't give you those instructions. You'd better answer the phone," Troy said flatly through gritted teeth while removing his jacket. His suspicions that Robert kept me on a short leash for personal reasons were becoming harder and harder for me to convince him otherwise.

I excused myself, finding a quiet spot to take the call.

Robert wanted me to come in an hour early tomorrow to go over some research before our staff meeting. When I hung up and returned to the table, Troy had finished my cocktail and seemed more relaxed.

"Can you ladies handle some shots?" Troy challenged the table, calling out to the bartender to bring over his best tequila.

"Whatever. How about, can *you* handle a shot?" I smarted off, kissing him on the lips as he pulled me close.

"Next time you better let your boss know you're off the clock, before I tell him. Man to man. I don't like how he tries to have all this power and control over you."

"You need to just worry about having control over your *own* woman," I playfully jabbed, stroking his face, kissing him again.

"Keep it up, and I will throw some of this control on you." Troy smiled, becoming aroused as I pressed my body against his.

"Do you guys need a room?" Tara teased as we all broke into laughter.

I lost track of time. About five shots later we had abandoned my girls, and we were in our own little world on the dance floor. A funky hip-hop track was bumping as Troy danced behind me. He began rubbing my thighs. I suddenly remembered I'd gone pantiless. Big deal. "Girlfriend" liked to be free every now and then too, especially in the summertime when I wore certain clingy fabrics.

In the clumsiness of tequila shots and Cosmos, I tried to

stop Troy's hand, but it was too late. His hand slipped under my dress. As he began to massage me, I felt myself having an orgasm on the dance floor. I excused myself and rushed into the ladies' room.

I had that drunken pounding-heart feeling. Had anyone seen my lewd act?

"Oh we saw it all!" Tara barreled into the bathroom.

"Everything! You two are wild!" Judy screeched. "We just came to tell you we're out. Not that you would notice."

We giggled, giving each other good-bye hugs and air smooches. When they were gone, I stared in the mirror for a moment. *Look out Lil' Kim!* I thought, hysterical with laughter.

I flung the bathroom door open and exited with my head held high. I scooped Troy by the arm, and we walked out of the bar and right into Randy Lanier.

"Whassup T? Lindsay?" Randy was so suave it made my stomach turn. He had that pretty, prep-boy look I was talking about. It was our first time seeing him since Troy and I started dating and you could feel the tension. My high was instantly blown.

"Whassup Randy!" Troy gave him a pound.

"Randy," I said, avoiding eye contact.

"Don't leave. Stay. Let's have some drinks. I know you like drinks, Lindsay!"

Randy wanted to make it clear we had history. "No, I'll pass." I ignored Randy and seductively pulled Troy close. "But you stay, honey."

"You sure?" Troy asked.

"Absolutely, have fun." I kissed him good-bye, wishing my girls were still here. I flipped my hair and strutted off Naomi Campbell style. I had to make sure my exit was memorable.

Chapter 8

Killer Dress

My wedding planning is in complete shambles!

Granny and my mother can't afford to fly down here every weekend to help me pick out my dress. It's bad enough I compromised with the entire family by having the ceremony in Buffalo. But I will not, I repeat *not* buy my wedding dress in Buffalo! Not when I live in the greatest fashion city in the world, second only to Milan.

Not to be misleading, Michael and I are far from rich. But this is my first and hopefully last time being a bride. I plan to have my nuptials in all the major publications back home and *Jet* magazine, and I plan on representing Buffalo well.

My dreams of becoming a famous writer haven't come to fruition just yet, but relocating to the city and getting married is considered success in the eyes of Buffalonians. So on that note, I *must* look the part. Never mind the fact that I've been driving poor Kyle insane with my indecisive dress antics.

"What about this one? I like the way the train detaches." Kyle held up what could have easily been gown number two thousand. Lord knows I've lost track.

"Yeah, it's nice but I don't know if I want my dress to be detachable!" I said, shuffling through Macy's bridal book. Kyle shot me a look and hung the dress back up, then continued to riffle though the endless racks of white.

"I have two words for you, *high maintenance*, and all I know is you better cut it out!" Kyle warned, but I knew better. Kyle was too happy to help me look for a dress. It took everything in him not to run into the dressing room and try one on himself.

"It's my wedding, so I'll complain if I want to," I said, playfully sticking my tongue out.

"I'm serious. This is our third store of the day. I mean, give me a break. I understand you want to look fabulous, but you know I know you. All of a sudden you want to turn into Miss Dainty. Hell, I can't even remember the last time I saw you in a dress. Trying to get all Miss America on me. Who do you think you are?" Kyle carried on. Although he wasn't really looking for an answer, something stirred inside me.

I was Charlie Thornton. I was a self-made beauty, and in the process of transformation from girl to woman I've become, shockingly, just what Kyle said, *high maintenance*. What's wrong with that? It's not the typical definition of "high maintenance": the mandatory weekly manicure, pedicure, and wax-me type. No, I'm the girl with slightly rough edges. Ashy hands, if I'm too busy for tedious moisturizing. Hairy legs in the summertime, if I don't feel like shaving. And maybe even chipped fingernail polish if I don't have time to make it to the nail shop.

That's who I am, but when I need to show it off, believe me, I know how! And for the first time in a long time, I feel good about myself.

Placing my hands on my hips I decided to let Kyle and the whole world know. "Well, mister, I'll tell you who I am. I'm one of the hottest new copywriters at my job. I have a man who wants to give me his last name, and although I'm thirty-two, I can still pull a twenty-year-old from all shades of the color spectrum. I'm all that *and* a bag of chips! That's who I am! So if I'm a little high maintenance, so be it. I have two words for you: *killer dress!*" I threw up my hands, making a grand exit.

"Oh no, Miss Thing didn't read me!" Kyle said, laughing as he ran to catch up with me.

I got home and the house was a mess, but thankfully silent. Michael had decided to treat the kids to Six Flags. They'd be at the amusement park till dusk. I had been complaining about my writer's block to Michael. So this morning, on my side of the bed, he left me a Giant Hershey's Kiss and a greeting card that read: *I love you a lot, and I hope some time alone will help lift your writer's block. The poem is lame maybe, because you're the writer of this family.*

I'm so lucky to be marrying a man who truly believes in me and my dreams. The card reminded me of when I first laid eyes on Michael. I was shopping in the NYU campus gift shop. I was taking a creative writing class to brush up on my skills, and Michael was completing his carpenter's license. He was looking for a birthday card for his mother and asked for my help. I suggested he get a blank card and write from his heart. When I told him I was a writer, Michael suggested I help him with the card in exchange for dinner. We've been inseparable ever since.

This morning was a disappointment as far as the dress hunt was concerned, but I had all afternoon to take another shot and work on my script.

I ran to my desk and decided to go back to an old ritual that my professor from NYU had passed on to me. I turned on the computer and printer. Professor Shepherd's method was to sit down with a printed copy of the script. This would allow the words to breathe and come to life, sparking a natural wave of what to write next. While the script was printing I could quickly tidy up the apartment, freshen up, and slip into some comfortable writing gear.

My favorite Diptyque candle was burning, and my sounds of nature CD played softly throughout the apartment, and I was on my third glass of Riesling. I was happily in the zone, sitting in the middle of the apartment surrounded by the pages from my screenplay that covered most of the floor. Suddenly, it came to me. I got it! I jumped up and sat down into my chair. *Act 5, scene 1 . . .* My fingers could barely keep up with the speed of my thoughts but I was on a roll.

Suddenly, the front door flew open, and terror invaded the room. MJ ran right over my papers, and I made a mad dive to protect what was left. "Damn it MJ, watch out!" And right out of a scene from *The Matrix*, out of the corner of my eye, in slow motion, Tiffany was running in and tripped on the cord to the computer. My heart stopped. I looked up, and the computer screen went black. "No!" I screamed as I tried to rescue the file, but it was too late, Act 5 was all gone.

Tiffany was on the ground holding her scraped knee and crying. Michael quickly picked her up, assessed the damage, and then walked over to me and kissed me on the forehead.

"I'm sorry babe, I love you," Michael said. "Listen, Little Man," he said to MJ, "you have to watch where you're going, okay?" MJ looked up at his dad and then at me, smiled faintly and said "Sorry." "Come on, MJ, help me get your sister ready for bed," Michael said while picking up the remaining papers from the floor. He turned back to me and whispered. "Right after I put them to bed, we'll tootsie roll all night, I promise."

Instantly my body warmed over. "All night?" I asked wantonly.

"All night," Michael said, discreetly sticking his tongue out at me, causing us both to laugh.

Chapter 9

Hot in Here

White sand, blue water, and a suite at La Sammana, St.-Martin's finest. Just what I needed for a weekend getaway. If Troy wasn't careful he was going to win my heart. He wasn't officially calling me his girlfriend, but we were doing all the things committed couples do and more. I'm loving everything about this man, especially his spontaneity.

When he called and asked me to join him in St.-Martin for his last day of shooting, I jumped on the last flight out of JFK. Alix Alexander's talent deal was closed, and Robert had given me the go-ahead to put the pilot script into development. Sam Finney, who'd won a Golden Globe for the box-office hit *High Octane*, was the writer. It was Friday, I had the weekend to let loose, and wouldn't have to miss a day of work.

Troy arranged for a car to pick me up from the airport. The limo entered the French side of St.-Martin, and calm washed over me as I took in the beauty of the island. When the car pulled up to the set, I heard Troy call out "Action!" I navigated my way through the cameras, lights, and electric cables, finding a spot with an empty chair to quietly observe.

I didn't want him to see me yet. I wanted to surprise him. I was so happy, watching him behind the camera monitor. I started daydreaming about the two of us being the next power couple on the cover of *Ebony* or our wedding being featured in *In Style*. For the first time a man was into my goals, aspirations, and dreams just as much as I was into his.

"And cut!" Troy directed the crew and extras.

As Troy was setting up for his last shot, I decided to call my sisters, Faith and Angie. They keep me grounded and live for my adventures. In exchange I get slice of domestic life. My three-way system worked like a charm when it came to putting my sister hotline in effect.

"Hey, Faith, it's me Lindsay. How do you feel? What's the latest from the doctor?" I said with an anxious tone.

"I'm feeling pretty good, just a little tired. They want me to start on steroids."

"Do you need anything?" I asked.

"I'll let you know. I want my doctor to check everything

out first. But enough of that. What's up? You sound like you've got some juicy news. I can hear it in your voice."

"I do! But hold on, I've gotta get Angie," I said, excitedly clicking over to call my other sister. She picked up on the first ring. "Hey, Angie. It's me and Faith." I was talking a mile a minute trying to get all the details out before the cameras started rolling again.

"I see you finally got some time for us little people," Angie snapped.

"Tell her, Angie." Faith just had to throw in her two cents. The older she got the more she acted like Mama.

"Spare me of all this bickering. Y'all, I'm in St.-Martin getting a fabulous tan. Troy flew me down for the weekend!" I shouted, almost forgetting I was on set. "I think I'm fallin' in love. He's the one, y'all!" I proclaimed.

"That's a wrap!" Troy announced. The crew gave a round of applause.

"I gotta go. Troy just finished shooting."

"Lindsay, take it slow and be careful!" Faith warned. "Call us when you get back. We love you!"

"And use a condom!" Angie added.

I closed my phone as Troy swooped in behind me, wrapping his arms around my waist.

"L, you ever been on a yacht?"

"L" was the pet name he started to call me. I liked that much better than Lin Lin.

His production company was having a white linen yacht party.

"I didn't bring anything to wear!" I said, panicked.

"So, let's go shopping."

Next thing I knew, Troy was walking me into Versace.

"L, check this out. This is hot. Try it on and put those shoes on too!"

The sales lady handed me a flowing backless slipdress, and I let the satin glide over my body, the bias cut clinging to my petite but shapely hips, accentuating the roundness of my behind. The low-cut neckline gave my C-cup all the justice it needed. I felt like Julia Roberts in *Pretty Woman*, parading around the store.

"You like it?" Troy asked.

"I love it!"

"Then it's yours."

"We also have it in pink and black," the sales lady added.

"She'll take all of them and the shoes too!" Troy shouted. My eyes widened.

"We also just got in some beautiful accessories. I think this one would really bring out the neckline," she said, handing me an ornate rhinestone choker.

"Just add it to the rest! Hook her up!" Troy said, dropping five grand as if it were nothing. Troy pulled me close and kissed me deep.

The Caribbean night breeze gently filtered through the seventy-foot luxury yacht *The Island Queen*. The setting was glamorously decorated with white sheers. Large throw pillows and mattresses were spread out on the upper deck and draped in white linen as well. Troy and I snacked on shrimp, caviar, and lobster, while a calypso band softly swooned.

With the waves crashing all around, we found our own

secluded corner of the boat. He sensually ran his fingertips over my eyelids, down my cheekbone, my neck, across my breasts. I felt my nipples hardening.

"You know what?" Troy said lightly, nibbling on my ear.

"What?" I said, smiling as Troy licked inside my ear, sending tiny goose bumps throughout my body. My breasts stood at full attention.

"Your breasts are my favorite," he said, caressing them. "And you know what else?"

"What?" My eyes were closed. My spine tingled.

"I want you, right here."

"Now?" I opened my eyes and looked around.

"Right now!" Troy gave me a deep long kiss.

It was time to give him all the goods. He had earned it and I was horny. He hiked the bottom of my dress up, slid a condom on, and wasted no time shimmying inside. I gave him all I had. I couldn't figure out who was outdoing the other. We both came so hard we almost passed out. Sex is so good when you haven't had it for a while.

Troy gently brushed my dress back down and inconspicuously zipped his linen slacks up. I was swooning. I couldn't blame my giddiness on alcohol. Not this time. I was sober and thinking as clear as the deep dark sky above me: I *am* falling. Hard.

We decided to relax on the cushions on the upper deck.

"You don't seem so stressed now, Lindsay Bradley," Troy softly said, placing my hand on his chest.

"I feel so much better now that I'm here with you. Work was wearing me out."

"That's because that fucking—" Troy's eyes narrowed.

"Robert just pushes me," I said, cutting him short. "And

I'm cool with it. But I won't be if he doesn't put my show into production and then hurry to get it on the air."

"Look, baby, you deserve the chance to produce that show. You're smart, resourceful, and one of the most creative people I know. As a matter of fact, I just got the news that I'm up for a huge Nike campaign. I really want to take the whole hip-hop thing to a new level. Got any suggestions?"

"Off the top of my head, you should go for hard-edged acoustic beats and strong visuals. I can see it now, it's gonna be the bomb!"

"Hold up! I haven't gotten it yet."

"But you will." I rolled over and kissed him.

"And you'll get your show, too," Troy said, hugging me.

With Troy there were no pretenses. I could be myself around him: silly and laugh-out-loud goofy, dancing around his apartment in a big T-shirt, imitating the latest dance craze—or be a hardball businesswoman who kicked butt and took names later. My future with Troy seemed assured and effortless.

Chapter 10

Operator . . . Can You Check This Line?

I can't believe how fast time flies, especially when you're supposed to walk down the aisle in less than six months. Christmas Eve is the day I'm to profess my love for Michael Rivera in front of two hundred guests. It's already July and I still haven't found that damn "killer dress"! I'm panicking because I used to complain that I didn't have enough time to look. That excuse doesn't work anymore. I have plenty of free time now with the kids being gone for the summer.

I pressed number one on the keypad, speed-dialing Granny.

"Hey, Granny."

"Hey, you must have been reading my mind. I was just about to call you. Sounds quiet over there," she said.

"Yes, Lord. The kids are still away visiting Juanita's mother in Florida for the summer. Her moving there was good timing. Michael and I lucked up by default."

We laughed.

"I went by the church today and Pastor Harris is pleased to have the ceremony there, especially with the new renovations." I could hear the delight in Granny's voice.

"That's great news," I said, growing more excited about my big day. Bethesda was a nondenominational church where I used to be a member. Now, I visit every chance I get when I go home for the holidays.

"Honey, wait until you see it. You know they moved the church to Main Street, the heart of the city." Granny was raving like she was preaching the gospel.

"Good, that makes for easy directions for my guests," I said.

"Yes, and you should see the skylight. Charlie, it's right in the front. I can see it now, as the guests are coming in, they'll look up and swear the snow is about to fall on them. That's how beautiful it is," Granny said, laughing to herself.

"Sounds beautiful." Just then the call waiting alerted me. "Granny hold on, that's my other line," I said before clicking over. "Hello?" I said, waiting to hear another voice. "Hello?" I asked again, hearing heavy breathing on the other end. "Hello!" I said, growing impatient. The caller hung up. Must've been a wrong number. I clicked back over to Granny.

"Granny, you still there?" I asked.

"Yes baby?"

"Granny, I still haven't found a dress."

"Charlie, please tell me you're kidding."

"No, I'm not, and trust me. I've been looking all over."

"I wish you would just listen to me and stop being so hardheaded. All you have to do is fly in for the weekend and we can go downtown to Brides R Us. I bet you'll find the perfect dress there. I see really nice ones in their commercials all the time." Granny didn't realize that her grandbaby was just a little bit too stuck-up for Brides R Us. The call waiting interrupted for the second time.

"Hold on Granny, it's my other line again," I said, checking the caller ID this time. It was a Manhattan area code. I remembered it was the same number that was on the caller ID screen when we returned from the Poconos. "Hello?" I said. There was no answer, and again I could hear someone breathing. "I know someone is there, I can hear you, jackass!" I was getting more agitated by the minute. "Hello?" Was this Juanita up to her old tricks again? Whoever it was knew they were working my nerves. On second thought, silence wasn't Juanita's style. "I don't know who this is, but call me when you have enough courage to open your mouth." I was using my hard-core Brooklyn voice. Clicking back over I was surprised to hear Granny wasn't on the line.

"Hey baby girl." It was my mother.

"Hi Mom. I was going to call you next," I lied.

I love my mother but sometimes she just gets under my skin. I have this thing about how she is and the type of men she goes after. Ever since she and my father got divorced some thirty years ago, it seems like my mother became terribly insecure.

The men she chooses to date are nowhere near the quality of man my father was. Don't get me wrong, my dad is no saint, but at least he's an educated, hardworking man who actually loved her. Now it seems like her only qualifications are: *Don't have a job; think you're fine; and think you're pimp-player of the year. FYI, I'm only interested if you can't do a damn thing for me.* That would be Mom's ad in the personals. I just hate this about her. I braced myself.

Beep! This time, I gladly welcomed call waiting.

"Mom, hold on, I have to get the other line." I clicked over. "Hello!" This time I snapped, ready for another match with the silent stalker.

"Hey sweetie, why are you screaming?" It was Michael.

"Oh, sorry baby. Somebody has been calling and not saying anything. What's up? I'm on the phone with the family."

"I was calling to let you know that I'm working another double shift. So if you haven't started already, don't cook. I'll grab something from the deli."

"Too late, I just finished. So, I guess I shouldn't wait up?"

"No, I'll be in late. I'll try to call you on my dinner break. All right, let me get back. Love you," Michael said, blowing me a kiss over the phone.

"Love you too," I said, clicking back over. "Ma?"

"Yeah, baby girl, I'm still here," my mother said.

"So what's up?" I asked.

"Well Jake and I went to the movies and he was looking too fine . . ."

Chapter 11

Hanging by a Thread

The sound of my clattering heels running up Troy's front steps could be heard a mile away. By the time I reached the door, I was breathless but happy and excited. Troy thought we were going out to dinner, but I had a better plan. Chinese takeout and a romantic evening at home.

His house had been the last fixer-upper to be sold in the quaint tree-lined Brooklyn Heights neighborhood. I called it his work-in-progress. Troy was still slowly pulling it all together, but I didn't care how it looked, as long as I was with *him*. And lately, that's all I'd been wanting.

Troy was expecting me and left the door unlocked. I collected myself and walked through the unfurnished house, carefully stepping over the workmen's gear scattered about. I could still hear the shower running. I quickly moved around in the kitchen grabbing plates and silverware, then rushed up the narrow staircase that connected the kitchen to the rooftop patio.

From Troy's Brooklyn Heights view, Manhattan's twinkling Lower East Side glistened off the not-so-distant East River. Troy stepped onto the patio with a big grin on his face.

"All this for me?"

"Yep."

"Any special reason?"

"Just because . . . "

Troy grabbed my hand and led me away from the table. I was facing the full moon as he slipped behind me, taking my forearms and stretching them out to the sides. The warm summer evening breeze ran over me.

Troy's large fingers fumbled with each delicate crystal button on my silk blouse. He turned me around and kissed my lips with his full mouth and lingered on the dimple in my chin, eventually making his way down to my breasts. He smiled. My Chantilly lace bra revealed just enough for a good imagination. "Firm, yet supple, like small ripe grapefruits, ready for the picking," Troy teased sexily, making me giggle.

He unhooked my bra and it floated to the ground. Then he unbuttoned my slacks, kissing the natural curve of my belly as they slid over my hips. He pulled me close. While touching my thighs and buttocks, Troy lifted his sweatshirt over his head, exposing his soft torso. My eyes met his tanned skin that still glowed from St.-Martin. He was all mine. Life couldn't get any better.

"You make me so happy, Troy," I whispered softly.

"Baby, so do you."

"No." I looked at him seriously. "I mean happier than I've ever been in my life."

"You're a good woman, Lindsay. I'm lucky to have you in my life."

I was overwhelmed with emotion. Could I have finally found my dream guy?

"I could stay with you like this forever," I hinted. Suddenly, my pager went off and I knew it could only be one person, Robert.

"Let me guess," Troy said with disgust.

"No, it couldn't be, it's too late," I said, looking at my watch.

"What's new? Why would tonight be any different than any other damn night." My pager buzzed again. "Just answer the damn thing!" Troy demanded as he stood up and walked into the house.

After I finished my call, I made sure I turned both the two-way and cell phone off. I couldn't afford any more interruptions.

Troy was seething as he downed his glass of Merlot. He felt, as always, that Robert intentionally interrupted us just to test his manhood. He tried his best to cover up his insecurity. But for months now, he's been referring to us as a threesome: me, Robert, and him.

At times like this, I feel conflicted. I want Troy to understand. Women don't normally have someone with stroke in the business looking out for their best interest.

"So, did you handle your business?" Troy said sarcastically. His voice echoed in the large empty room.

"Robert just needed some quick info."

"*He* needed? I'm sick of what he needs. You're mine after work hours, on weekends and holidays! He's pushing my buttons and disrespecting me by intruding on my territory!"

I poured on the charm, and another glass of wine to calm him. "I promise to talk to Robert first thing in the morning. I'm gonna tell him he better stop, before I have my man beat him up!" I teased, kissing Troy's neck, his weak spot, making him give in.

Troy gripped my thighs. His fingers snatching hold of my panties, pulling them down. I clawed his back as he carried me up the small winding staircase. Troy laid me across the futon. I felt for Troy. The silky wetness between my legs excited him. He grew harder and larger. With each thrust, I became more and more overcome with emotion. I loved this man and wanted the world to know. I couldn't stop shaking as I started to come down. Troy quietly grunted with satisfaction. He wrapped his arms around me, as if he would never let go. My whole life I'd dreamed of being held like this.

"Troy?" I said, burying my face in his chest.

"Yeah, L?"

"I just wanted to tell you how much I . . ." I paused. My heart was moving faster than my brain and I couldn't believe

I was about to tell Troy those three magic words. A sudden fear of rejection made me rethink. "I love being with you."

"Me too," Troy mumbled, half asleep.

The next morning while Troy finished dressing, I paced the kitchen floor, rehearsing my memorized lines. I wasn't going to let another day go by without telling him.

Troy was concentrating on shots and angles for his first national commercial in L.A. He stuffed his camera lens and other last-minute items into a leather duffle. If I didn't say it now I might not have the courage again. A horn blew. The car service was outside waiting. I poured a cup of coffee.

"Troy?"

"Yeah, L?" He was patting his jacket pockets. "You seen my cell?"

Pointing to it on the counter, I grabbed his arm with my free hand.

"I'm really going to miss you, Troy. I'm so proud of you getting the Nike campaign."

"Thank you, baby."

The car horn sounded again. "Baby, I gotta go." I clenched his arm. "Troy, I just wanted you to know," I swallowed hard, "I love you." Troy froze. He leaned down slowly and kissed me on the forehead like a puppy, and whispered, "Don't forget to lock up, Lindsay. I'll call you." Troy walked out, leaving me standing in the kitchen, clad only in my underwear, holding a piping hot cup of coffee.

I struggled desperately to hide an oncoming anxiety attack. Frantic and unsure thoughts bounced around in my head, while butterflies danced a light salsa in my stomach. I checked my phone, no messages, and nervously ran my fingers through my limp hair.

My behavior all boiled down to Troy. I hadn't seen or heard from him since the morning I told him I loved him almost two weeks ago. I chalked the first few days up to the possibility that I'd simply scared him. How could he just kiss me and walk out the door like nothing happened, like I'd just said, "Looks like rain today, better carry an umbrella." Not even a "Thank you very much, but no thanks" or a "Gee, what a nice surprise."

I hadn't been able to get him or that day off my mind. I've even tried to bury myself in the Alix Alexander project. Robert keeps catching simple mistakes in the script that I should've noticed, but I'm distracted thinking about Troy. I haven't had much sleep, and I've got to pull it together.

Today's staff meeting had been a disaster. I excused myself and ran out of the conference room midsentence in front of my entire department. *How could that be?* Lindsay Bradley was always in control, a perfectionist. Thank God I was hidden behind the walls of my cubicle and no one could see me cry.

I peered out from my Times Square perch. New York was a living, breathing museum. Neon flashed even in broad daylight. Everything moving in various directions, the bird's-eye view seemed to be a splattered patchwork of Basquiat. But the sight was somehow soothing for my troubled mind. Today, I wanted to be an unknown piece of the human jigsaw puzzle below too.

I'd left messages for Troy at work, home, and on his cell. I even had a crystal bowl of floating white roses from the

Daily Blossom waiting at his office the day he was scheduled to return from his shoot. Whatever was going on with Troy, I couldn't call again. Damn it! I could hear Robert's footsteps heavy and sure coming toward me. I tried to arrange myself in a more confident posture. The look in my eyes was far from the commanding certainty I normally felt.

I'd left Robert to clean up the mess from the meeting, and he was furious. He whipped around my cubicle wall.

"What the hell was that show all about, Lindsay?"

"I'm sorry Robert," I stuttered.

"Sorry? Listen, if you weren't ready for this kind of responsibility you should've told me a long time ago." He didn't care that the entire staff could hear him yelling.

I stiffened, hoping I wouldn't be completely humiliated. "I want to," I said, clearing my throat. "I mean I *am* ready."

"Well, act like it!"

Robert's words were trapped in my ears like standing water. I couldn't hold up any longer. My mouth felt like sticky gauze on an open wound. Robert turned his back to me, facing outside, and continued his rant.

"You've been off your game for over a week now. If I have to step in and do your job, then you don't need that nice big check I'm paying you each week," Robert growled.

What I really needed was some water, but I was afraid to get up for fear both legs would give way.

"Is it something in your personal life? Do you need time off?" he drilled, though I felt a hint of sarcasm in his tone.

"Robert, I'll get it together," I said, trying my best to get my words out.

"Then you better dig in and do just that. It's about focus!"

After that I swear I didn't hear a word he was saying. I think he was preaching one of his favorites. Sermon #202 about the goals of the company and the responsibilities of its executives. My brain felt like it would implode at any minute. I really needed some air.

Robert stopped ranting, looked down, and suddenly noticed my state. "Lindsay are you all right?" His slightly weathered face zoomed toward mine. "Can you hear me?" Robert said, shaking me. "Somebody bring her some water," he barked.

I snapped out of it. The last thing I wanted was for the paramedics to come. "I'm okay," I said, squinting.

Robert placed the glass of water gently in my hands. I couldn't gulp fast enough. I cleared the lump lodged in my throat.

"I swear I'm fine. I think I'm just coming down with the flu, and need to go home."

Robert softly patted my shoulders and helped me up.

"I don't want you driving. Take a car service and call me if you need anything."

I made my way into the ladies' room and ran my fingers through my hair again, shaking the morning out. I rinsed water over my face, pursed my lips, and frowned. Two vertical lines cut between my thinly arched eyebrows. I tied my hair in a high bun, and collected myself for the last time.

Chapter 12

The Village

I was twenty minutes late meeting Kyle on Sixth Avenue in front of Pizzeria Uno—what's come to be our regular meeting spot since Kyle started helping with my wedding errands. He thinks I don't know why he chose this location. A few blocks south are the basketball courts, and in the summertime on most days you'll find Gotham's best selection of men there. Kyle is always on time and since his subway exit is right across from the courts, he can sneak all the eye candy he desires. I'm sure that's why he always gets here extra early.

I was speed-walking up the block. Kyle gave me an exaggerated glare.

"I'm so sorry I'm late, Kyle," I said apologetically.

"Save it, I'm PMSing, Miss Honey, and we've got way too much to do, so let's move it," Kyle said, switching off up Eighth Street, dragging me along.

"Remind me again, Bridezilla, exactly what are we looking for today?" Kyle asked, checking out the male flavor walking about.

"Gifts for my bridesmaids. I want them to be one of a kind, something you can only find in New York."

"Sounds like a job for the flea market on Fourth Street," Kyle declared.

The flea market was an open lot full of vendors that sold just about everything from T-shirts, CDs, and antiques to jewelry and bongs. You name it, they've got it. The best part about the market is that most of the vendors make their own merchandise. And—one of the beauties of New York—the price is always negotiable!

"Charlie, you're going to love me. I think I've found what you're looking for," Kyle said, holding up a handmade black beaded ring with a ruby-colored center.

"Look at how elaborate the detail is," I said, putting it on.

"Look at the others." Kyle pointed. "They're similar but no one ring's exactly like the other."

"Kyle they're perfect!" I grabbed seven rings. I only needed six for my wedding party. I had a thing for one-of-a-kinds, the extra one was mine.

"How much?" I asked the vendor. When she said six dollars each I was tempted to haggle, but the craftsmanship was worth so much more. I was already getting a bargain.

"Great! I'll take all of them." I gladly paid her. "Thank you, Kyle!" I grabbed Kyle by the arm and kissed him on the cheek.

"You're welcome. Lord knows I couldn't handle another diva episode." Kyle rolled his eyes at me.

We headed to our favorite, Frutti D'Mare. It was a cute sidewalk café with a traditional Italian décor that made it both romantic and friendly. Their antipasti and lasagna made you say to hell with a low carbs diet! We were regulars, so the hostess seated us quickly.

After our main course and second glass of wine, I felt it was time for me to come clean with Kyle. Part of this meeting was to find gifts for my bridesmaids. The other part was to get some advice. Something had been bugging me all week, a problem I hadn't told anyone yet.

"Kyle, I want to talk to you about something. But promise not to get all dramatic," I said, shooting him a serious look.

"I promise. Talk to me," he said.

I took a deep breath and started. "Someone has been playing on my phone. At first they called and just held the line, or hung up when they heard my voice. But lately they've gotten really bold. Yesterday when I answered, the woman called me a bitch and hung up."

"Humph!" Kyle said, giving a disgusted look. "Go on," he said, insisting I spill it.

"Well, I think it has something to do with Michael."

"You know damn well it has something to do with his sneaky ass!" Kyle rolled his head and neck.

"Kyle, you promised," I pleaded.

"I'm sorry but I knew he would do this again. I told you, once a cheat always a cheat!" Kyle loudly whispered.

"I said I *think* it has something to do with him. I did not say I *know*," I retorted, signaling him to lower his voice.

"Yeah, just like you didn't know two years ago," Kyle huffed.

"Yeah and I kicked him out!"

"For one day!" Kyle reminded.

"I never had proof, and besides we weren't engaged then," I said defensively.

"So what's that supposed to mean?" he questioned. I was silent. "That's what I thought. All I want to know is what are you going to do?" Kyle folded his arms.

"First, I'm not going to assume."

"Does the number come up on your caller ID?" he drilled.

"Yes, and I think I wrote it down, too," I said.

"Good! So, when are you going to call it? Or do you want me to call the skank?" Kyle said, challenging me.

"See, I knew I should have kept this to myself."

"No, because deep down you know that Michael is not the one for you. I've told you this before. You're my girl so I've tried to be there for you. You know I never trusted the—" Kyle was in rare form.

"Kyle, chill!" I said, cutting him off. "I'm still marrying the man and you're going to be there. So don't say anything you might regret."

"Fine, but you better call that damn number. And think about this: if you find out he is cheating, are you still going to marry him? That's all I want to know!" Kyle said, waiting for my answer.

"Like I said, it could be anybody," I said, avoiding the question.

"That's not what I asked. I asked, if you're right are you going to marry him?" Kyle wouldn't let it go.

"Kyle, of course not!" I answered, not quite sure if I was being honest with Kyle or myself.

Chapter 13

A Little Color
in My Life

I'd done a decent job getting things back on track in the office after what happened last week. At least, a good enough job to fool Robert. After work, I needed to keep my mind occupied. I figured I'd catch a sale. There were bills to pay, but considering my mental state, one or two bills might have to wait. I had retail therapy to do.

Fifth Avenue's marvelous display of Tiffany, Gucci, Prada, and Cartier was a playground for the wealthy. Although I wasn't wealthy, it was cool to dream.

Henri Bendel's always felt like Christmas to

me, even on blazing summer days, decorated with its glistening, shiny cosmetic counters.

I made my way to the scarf case. I wanted to feel pretty. And there they were! Yellows, reds, blues, oranges, purples—silk and Chanel! I quickly yanked my scrunchy off, tying the scarf pirate style with my hair hanging beneath. I stood at the mirror, pleased. I whipped out my wallet and gladly paid the petite, stylishly dressed saleslady behind the counter. She handed me the signature brown and white striped Bendel bag.

I strutted out regally through the oversized doors. Sometimes all you need is some color in your life . . . and some sisterly advice.

"Hello? Faith, it's me Lindsay. Hold on, I'm calling Angie."

I clicked twice, connecting all three of us.

"Hey Angie, it's me and Faith." I couldn't wait to let loose, but Angie beat me to it.

"Mama asked me if I'd spoken with you. I told her that I left you a message *three* days ago. I knew you'd call sooner or later," Angie scolded.

"Tell her, Angie!" Faith said.

"Would the two of you shut up and listen. This is my dime and I really need your advice!" I shouted, forgetting I was on a public street. "I've got issues!" I was about to have a meltdown all over again.

"It's about that man you're seeing?" Angie smarted.

"Troy hasn't hurt my baby sis, has he?" Faith questioned.

"Y'all, I haven't heard from Troy since I told him I loved him the morning he left town to go on his big shoot." My voice trailed off. I was embarrassed.

"What!" they screamed.

While Faith ranted, Angie just kept the "Umph, umph, umphs" going.

"Lindsay, it's cardinal rule number one not to tell a man you love him before he says it to you. I know how you like to be in control, but let the man be the man. Put a cap on your emotions and let him take charge. You need to let Troy start making more of an effort and if he doesn't, so what! A man will come. Just concentrate on your career." Suddenly, I heard a loud crash in the background. "Hey! I said cut it out. You are too big to be jumping on his back like that!" Faith yelled, shattering our eardrums. "Don't have kids! Y'all, I've gotta go, my husband's home. Love you and remember what I said, Lindsay." Faith hung up to rush to her son's rescue.

Angie kept right on talking. "Anyway . . . Lindsay, I can understand why you told him you loved him. Believe me, all the fancy gifts and sweet talk. Humph! That man just has you turned out on his game. Forget about him! But I gotta get to Boy Scouts. Call me later. Love you!"

"Love you too," I said, disconnecting the call.

I heard both Angie's and Faith's messages loud and clear, but their advice was easier to hear than apply.

Just as I looked up, a taxi came to a screeching halt and out jumps Troy's friend Paris. Paris is sexy in an earthy kind of way, with short dreads and full beard. He greets me with a muscular hug and I decided to pass on the available cab to chat. Maybe I'd get a clue about what was going on with Troy.

"What's up, Lindsay? You look great, as usual," he tells me.

"Thanks, you're looking pretty good too," I say as I give him a coy grin.

"My boy T did his thing landing that Nike commercial. That's some major paper." Paris was obviously in a talking mood and I intended to take full advantage of it.

"Yeah, I'm proud of him."

"Me and a few of the boys took him out to celebrate last week when he got back from L.A. We got faded!"

Troy always complained about Paris's big mouth, but I was appreciating it this time. "Oh, that's nice." I hope he couldn't tell I was getting a bit nervous.

"Great to see you, Lindsay, I'll tell T I ran into you," Paris says and gives me a hug good-bye.

"Yeah, you do that," I said, serving up a fake smile and wishing I had a magic wand to do an abracadabra and vanish.

Chapter 14

A Train:
Next Stop Reality

I'd waited weeks for my 4:30 meeting with Miranda but it was worth it. I was prepared. Everyone else on the account had gotten a bonus except me. I was going to go in there and come out with everything I deserved, or I was headed straight for Johnnie Cochran's office.

"I'm sorry, Charlie. I totally forgot to e-mail you. Miranda needs to reschedule," said Miranda's assistant, Karen, barely looking up from her computer.

"Karen, you pass by my office every time you go to the ladies' room, couldn't you have told me earlier?" I was getting the runaround, and *she* knew that *I* knew Miranda was purposely dodging me.

"I'm really sorry, but Miranda has already left for the airport. She has a meeting in L.A. tomorrow." Karen was the gatekeeper and there was no sense in battling.

"Fine, then can you please put me in for her next available appointment?" I said, trying to collect myself.

"No problem, but I have to speak with Miranda first," Karen said, expressionless.

I dragged myself back to my office and, when I opened the door, saw that Kyle was waiting inside.

"What are you still doing here?" I asked.

"How did the meeting go?" Kyle gave a concerned look.

"It was canceled, long story. What's up? You look like something's wrong."

"Listen, Charlie, I know I was hard on you about Michael. Don't listen to me. I'm just bitter about my own shit," Kyle said, hinting he had a problem and needed an ear.

"Why don't we walk to the subway station together and we can talk more," I said, closing my office door. Since my big meeting had been canceled, why shouldn't I leave a little early?

As we made our way to the train, Kyle told me all about a man he'd met online. They had e-mailed back and forth for a few weeks and finally decided to meet.

"So I show up but there's no mystery man. I told him what I would be wearing and gave him a description so that he could find me. But I think he saw me and decided I wasn't fine enough so he left," Kyle said disappointedly.

"You do know it's his loss," I said, giving him an encouraging squeeze and a kiss.

"You think?"

"I *know.*"

"I knew you'd make me feel better! Ooh, I swear, Charlie, men are so shady out here. I think that's why I was so quick to jump on Michael's case and I was wrong. You've got a good hardworking brother, because honey, I've seen the way he treats you. Flowers and everything." Kyle stopped and grabbed my hand. "I wish I had a man like Michael."

"Kyle, I know Michael loves me, but that doesn't make him innocent." I started thinking about the harassing phone calls again and all the double shifts Michael had been working lately.

"Trust your gut, but don't get sucked into my bitterness or anybody else's. If Michael is doing wrong, karma will catch him. Okay!" Kyle gave two finger snaps and a circle.

"You're right about that, and don't worry, Kyle, your Mr. Right is out there, and you'll find him," I said as we reached the subway station.

"Yeah, well, in the meantime you go home and make love to that man of yours. Get a yell in for me too, honey!"

"You're a character!" I laughed as Kyle blew me a kiss.

I ran down the subway stairs, feeling and smelling the blowing wind, a sure sign that a train was coming. I skipped the last two steps and landed solidly on both feet. A jazz trio played a spicy "Girl from Ipanema." The tired booth operator wearing a bright blue wig popped her fingers to the beat. I breezed past, tossing a handful of loose change into the musician's money hat, because he was doing the song proud. I quickly slid my Metro card through the machine, amazed it worked on the first try. I pushed through the dull chrome turnstile and jumped onto the platform, just as the doors of the A train opened.

"Yes!" I said, squeezing myself into the train. The patrons were packed in like sardines.

Hopefully, there wouldn't be any train delays, and I would beat Michael home, take a shower, and cook his favorite meal: pan-fried chicken breast, homemade mashed potatoes, and French-style green beans. Thank God I remembered to defrost the chicken.

"Next stop . . . Utica Station!"

The muffled mixture of the conductor's voice and heavy static blared from an old worn-down intercom. The newly renovated station, freshly painted in red, black, and white, was coming into view. I was pressed up against the doors. When the subway car stopped, I flew out, running up the steps.

"Renovation my ass! How about putting in a friggin' escalator!" I announced. My heart was beating so fast I had to rest for a minute when I got to street level, but I was rejuvenated by the thought of the much-needed lovemaking session I was planning for my baby and me. I decided to stop wasting time and energy thinking about a bunch of unvalidated suspicions. I smiled and headed home.

"Damn it!" I yelled, dropping my keys, rushing to get inside. The apartment was still. I turned the lights on. It was just like I had left it that morning, immaculate and intact. "No kids, no kids, no kids!" I chanted as I ran into the laundry room, peeling off every article of clothing except my bra and panties, and throwing them into the corner hamper.

I'd had one hellacious day. I walked into the kitchen, automatically opened the refrigerator to pull out the chicken. Hell no! I stopped myself and reached for a beer instead. Yeah, one of Michael's favorites, Heineken. To tell the truth, I didn't feel like cooking a damn thing. I popped the cap and took a hard swig. What the hell am I breaking my back to be Donna Reed for? It would be nice if Michael offered to take me out to dinner for a change, or run me a hot bath after a rough day at the office.

I plopped down on the sofa, still in my underwear, and polished off the entire beer. The more I thought about Miranda having the nerve to put me off for the fourth damn time like I'm unimportant, the more I wanted to go and get another beer. I decided against it. Beer got me drunk fast, and I was already feeling a little buzzed.

Michael would be home soon. At least I hoped he would. He'd been working *a lot* of overtime and needed a hot meal, me too for that matter. Cooking helps me release tension, anyway. Instead of having another drink I'd take my anger out on the pots. It was final. I would get in that kitchen and cook us up the best damn dinner we've ever had.

I threw the pots and pans onto the stove. I was good at multitasking, so while the food was cooking, I rushed back into the laundry room and finished undressing. As I turned to exit the room, I took a moment to notice the cute but tiny space. I smiled, thinking back to the day Michael walked me in here blindfolded, and when he removed the blindfold, surprise crept over my face, from ear to ear.

Michael had turned this nothing, cubbyhole of a room into a walk-in closet haven and laundry room. Before I left for a long weekend in Buffalo, I saw a floor display at Bed, Bath & Beyond and fell in love with it. It had a mesh wall and hanging racks, a canvas hamper, and lots of utility shelves. Michael copied it exactly. He could be so thoughtful when he wanted to.

I took a long hot shower so I could be fresh for my baby. I was looking forward to a little tootsie rollin'. The food was done and I set the table. I slipped into one of Michael's favorite Victoria's Secret teddies, and topped it off with their signature pear body spray. The house was lit with scented candles, and the bed was fitted with satin sheets instead of the usual cotton. I laid down across the bed in a sexy come-and-get-it pose, rehearsing how I was going to look when my man walked through the door.

I was interrupted by the ringing telephone. *Let the machine answer*, I thought. But what if it was Michael?

"Hello?" I said, putting my hand on my hip. I just knew it better not be Michael calling to say he was working another double.

"You must think you're really special? Well you're not, bitch!" my stalker threatened.

I hurried and dialed star sixty-nine, but was defeated when I heard the recorded operator politely say, *"The number you are trying to call cannot be reached by this method."*

What is going on? I clenched the phone tight. I adjusted the tension in my neck and shoulders. This is some bullshit. I hung up the phone and leaned against the wall in frustration. I didn't need anything else fucking up my day. Who kept calling? And did the calls have something to do with Michael? Before I let my mind go completely wild I realized that I was tired, hungry, and in desperate need of some loving from my man. The thought of the much-needed lovemaking session with Michael quickly rejuvenated me. I decided to pull a Scarlett O'Hara and worry about the phone calls tomorrow. For now, I'd focus on tonight's plan.

I must have fallen asleep, because when I rolled over Michael was in bed snoring! I sat up and looked over at the clock. It was 5:30 A.M. Had I dreamed the whole thing? The phone calls? The cooking? Everything? I got out of bed and went into the kitchen. The table was still set for two, only one plate was missing and the pots and pans were stored away in the refrigerator. I walked over to the sink and saw one dirty dish, a fork, and one glass. I couldn't believe my eyes. I couldn't believe the son-of-a-bitch had had the nerve to eat, and hadn't bothered to wake me up! Couldn't he see what I'd planned? Now that I thought about it, when I woke up I had been lying on top of the sheets, but Michael was underneath them.

I walked back into the bedroom, and stood in the doorway watching Michael sleep. Maybe if I stared at him long enough, I'd telepathically find out what was really going on.

So many questions ran through my mind. Why was this woman calling me? *Who* was the woman who called earlier this evening? What time had Michael gotten home? Why was all this happening right before our wedding? I was suddenly flooded with insecurity as I stared at Michael, who, unlike me, was at peace and asleep. I tried hard, but I couldn't hold back. Tears gushed from my eyes.

Chapter 15

The Lion's Den

I didn't know just how serious Judy was until she sent both Tara and I formal e-mail invitations for our "Supper Club" night. When there was a new hot restaurant that had the city buzzing, we showed up to be the "chic critique" patrol. Bond Street, the swanky new place for sushi, was the choice tonight.

I was the first to arrive. Anxious all day, I needed Tara and Judy's advice on how to deal with Troy. I wanted to see him so badly. I was on the verge of doing something drastic.

"Lindsay sweetie!" Judy's way of greeting a

person was like the sticky sweetness of wet cotton candy on a humid summer day.

A young, dapper host escorted us through Bond Street's unique trilevel design. An elevator was our chariot to the third-floor dining room. Bond Street's modern décor was minimalist and I rated it an A plus just for style.

"I'll have the salmon roll, a miso soup, the house salad, and some plum wine." The waiter quickly jotted down the order as Judy shut the menu and then just as quickly, she opened it again. Judy firmly believed that it was more than a woman's prerogative to change her mind, it was her genetic right. This was the torturous and painstaking part of our supper club. "Wait! That may be too fishy."

"Ya think? It's only a sushi bar," I snapped.

Judy finally decided that she'd made the right choice and we got on with the night.

"So what's the 411 ladies?" Judy challenged.

"Something is seriously wrong with Troy and me."

"Oh, please, that Negro isn't going anywhere. He loves your dirty drawers." Judy grimaced. Tara nudged her.

"Lin Lin, what's going on?" she frowned.

"I think it has something to do with me telling him I loved him."

"Bad move!" Judy threw her hands up.

"Judy, shut up!" I yelled.

Tara put her arm around my shoulder. "Sweetie, it's okay. Just lower your voice. Don't forget where we are." She nervously looked around the room before turning back to me. "Lin Lin, when did this happen?"

"Girl, it was weeks ago, when he left for L.A."

"Why didn't you tell us?" Judy asked.

"We're your best girlfriends. We're here for you."

"I've just been so stressed and busy with preproduction, not to mention the fact that we've all been playing phone tag. I wasn't about to leave something as important as this on an answering machine or two-way."

"Lindsay, I'm sorry, but you can't shock that kind of man with an announcement like that. You'll just send him running into the arms of some lucky chickenhead," Judy whispered, aghast.

"Okay, so how do I fix it? What do I do now? I haven't talked to him or seen him in two weeks." I wanted to hear answers fast.

"Lin Lin, you have to do everything in your power to make him feel comfortable again and let your little announcement blow over," Tara insisted.

"When you do see him or talk to him, act like nothing's changed, and don't ever bring that day up again," Judy jumped in and was on a roll.

"Maybe this is a sign. You know, he's never even officially called me his girlfriend," I mentioned.

"Lin Lin, what's in a name or a title? You guys have been inseparable for over four months. Everyone knows you're a couple," Tara said firmly.

Maybe my girls were right. Persistence is what's gotten me everything else in life and I had to attack this situation with Troy the same way.

A few hours later, I wasn't feeling as hopeful or confident. I was swallowed up in a thick down comforter and the massiveness of my California King sleigh bed, going cross-eyed trying to read what was now our third rewrite of the pilot. Robert was driving the writer and me crazy with all his changes to the script. He's really testing my relationship with Finney, who was ready to quit after the second revision. *I can't take it anymore!* I thought, tossing the script to the side as I looked over at the nightstand at a picture of Troy and me. I needed to be held, but all I could do was ball up in the fetal position and cry.

I couldn't stop sobbing as I looked at photos of me and Troy. We looked so good together, and thinking about St.-Martin made me cry harder. I punched the pillows in frustration, and frantically began ripping the pictures up one by one.

After several minutes, I stopped crying and slowly slinked out of bed and grabbed the cordless. It was too late to call my sisters. Why bother? They wouldn't do anything but tell me how crazy I was to still be thinking about Troy. I needed to get myself together, and quick. I decided to take a long hot bath.

Forty-five minutes later, I stepped out of the tub and poured sesame-scented oil over my body, letting the moisture soak deep into my pores. I lit a Mandarine Votivo candle, releasing the mellow citrus fumes.

Then the phone rang. I skipped excitedly into the bedroom to answer it, hoping I'd conjured up Troy.

"Hello?"

"Hey, it's me."

I knew exactly who "me" was. It was my ex-beau Randy Lanier. I should've known it would only be a matter of time before he called after seeing Troy and me together. His ego had gotten the best of him.

"Lindsay, I think it's about time I get things right with you."

"Why, Randy? Why now? After all, I tried to remain friends, but you weren't interested."

"Okay, you're right. I was hurt, and I don't want to be childish anymore. So please accept my apology and just meet me for a drink."

"It's late, Randy. What's the catch?" I was suspicious. I *know* he wasn't trying to engineer a booty call.

"I'll cut right to it. You got my boy's head all messed up, so let me show you how much I care about both of you. Lindsay, let me help."

It was only eleven o'clock and I was curious about what he had to say. Randy's offer was too good to pass up; he had information and I needed it.

"Okay, Randy, but I want to be home by one." I didn't want to seem too anxious.

"Thank you so much, Lindsay. See you at Eros, Fifty-eighth and First. I'm headed there now, but take your time."

Before I could catch him to suggest another spot, he hung up. Eros was where Randy and I had had our first date. What was he really up to?

I opened my closet unsure of what would be appropriate to wear. I wanted to look good so he would report back to Troy. I thought back on the day I met him.

In the winter of 1998, I was coming off a dating dry spell and had been invited by a coworker to a dinner party Randy was hosting at his Manhattan loft. Randy's place was nestled in the hip and pricey Chelsea area.

When I arrived I scoped out the ultra-stylish, ethnically mixed crowd. The women and men dressed in clean lines, too busy trying to keep up with the Joneses to have a good time. Cigarette smoke thickened the room, and the attitude was very European. Randy sensed my uneasiness and paid special attention to me for the rest of the evening, getting me drinks and food.

We quickly became friends and bedmates. I fell into the flow of attending Randy's regular dinner parties. He called them "Big Willies on the Rise." I enjoyed the elaborate affairs at first. The guests included a selective, intimate group of New York's young sophisticates, handsome brothas with high incomes, flanked by gorgeous women.

After a while, I figured out the scene. All the women had been Randy's bedmates at one time or another too. I was always placed at the head of the table, because I was the flavor of the month, but he'd flirt with all the exes right in front of me. Eventually, I had had enough. I wanted a real relationship and decided to look elsewhere, and I wanted to get as far away from Randy as possible.

Tonight, I decided on a conservative but flattering black, long-sleeve Diane von Furstenberg wrap dress and pointy-toed slingbacks. I scooped up my keys, a small clutch, and was out the door and speeding out of the garage before I knew it.

As I entered Eros the aroma of Greek spices tantalized my senses. The overhead tented ceiling, low tables, and crescent-shaped booths, accented by decorative fringed pillows, turned the place into a miniature Athens.

"Boo!" Randy had me by the waist and I almost jumped

out of my skin as he snuck up beside me. I playfully shoved him. "Are you crazy?" I said.

"I forgot how jumpy you are. Good to see you're still looking good." Randy had a way of licking you with compliments and charm.

"What did you expect?" I returned.

"Chill, Lindsay," Randy said as he sneaked a kiss on my neck and led me to our waiting table. I was uncomfortable and not sure how to react. Randy was in an all-black Prada button-down dress shirt and flat-front slacks, black Prada loafers. He was impeccable.

"You hungry?" he asked.

"I didn't come to eat, Randy. I came to talk about Troy."

"Lindsay stop being a hard-ass. Let's break bread and then we'll talk."

I knew Randy well enough to know that he wasn't going to open his mouth if things didn't at least appear to go his way. "Fine. Then just some dessert. I ate earlier."

Give somebody like Randy an inch, and you know the rest. He had to have a four-course meal and two drinks before he was ready to talk. I'd had a drink and a half and was much more relaxed.

"So what's up, Randy? What's going on with Troy?" He knew I was pressed.

"Oh yeah, T. Listen, I hate how things turned out between us, Lindsay."

"It was never going to work with us, Randy. You could never give me what I needed, a commitment."

"You know Troy hasn't given you that either. C'mon

Lindsay, be truthful with yourself." Randy was using reverse psychology, and I was too dumb to pick up on it. "How could he? He's supposed to be my boy—no, my best friend—and look what he did to me. First he took you and now he's fucking my girl Robin!"

"You're lying, Randy. Coming here was a mistake." I grabbed my clutch and started to leave. Randy stopped me.

"Lindsay, I'm sorry to bring you bad news. I don't want to see you hurt like this."

"You couldn't have possibly thought hearing this was going to make me feel good!" I was shaking with anger, standing at the edge of the table.

"I know I should've warned you all the other times T messed around on you, but I was too angry to confront you. It was like I wanted him to cheat on you. I'm so sorry." Randy put his head down. "Now I see I was wrong."

I slowly sat down. I felt like my teeth had been kicked out and I burst into tears.

I didn't even know how long I had been crying when Randy wiped my eyes with the palms of his hands. "I'm sorry, Lindsay."

"No, I'm sorry, Randy."

"I know I was mad at you for a long time, but you didn't deserve this." Randy touched my face. "T could never understand how special you are."

Randy ordered the Shi-sha pipe, and the smoke from the apple-flavored tobacco intensified the alcohol in my system. High, drunk, and feeling good, Randy began to rub my thighs.

"That was a long time ago," I said sloppily, pushing his hand away.

"I still wish I had you, Lindsay."

"You wouldn't know what to do with it, Randy."

"I knew then, and I know even better now."

I rolled my eyes. I wasn't ready for this. Why was I still here? Randy leaned over and kissed the nape of my neck. I jerked away.

"I gotta go," I said.

"All I want to do is take away the pain T has caused you," Randy said, turning my face toward his.

Eyes were my weakness. His sad eyes and eyelashes that looked like feathers pulled me in.

"You know you really hurt my feelings when you stopped speaking to me, Randy. Things should've never gotten that ugly."

"I told you I'm sorry, and I won't ever hurt you again. I just want to please you," he whispered.

I moved closer to him and let all my defenses down and kissed him. Randy held me close, savoring me.

We tripped out the door, and slid into a waiting car. My plan to be home by one o'clock was shot, and I didn't even bother getting my car out of the parking garage.

Randy's apartment was dark. He lit a candle, and in the glow of the flame he leaned in to kiss me again. He gently untied my dress. It slithered down my body onto the floor. Randy guided me to his room, and even though Randy had told me things I didn't want to hear, Troy had hurt me deeper than any man. I wanted to strike back!

Randy opened his pants and pressed me against the wall. He slipped a condom on and entered me. The room was spinning. I hadn't remembered him being this big. He began forcefully shoving himself deeper and deeper inside.

We weren't making love. He was taking all his anger out on me. I screamed in pain. Randy covered my mouth.

"Shut up, and take it!" With each stroke, in and out, I got more and more dizzy. "You like it, don't you?"

"No, Randy," I mumbled, sobering up, trying to squirm away from his fully erect penis.

"What did I just tell you?" He smacked me hard on the thigh.

"Stop, Randy, I don't want to." Tears began to stream down my face. "Please, just stop." I pushed him back.

Randy looked at my tear-streaked face. I was naked and trembling. He was breathing heavy with his shirt open, chest exposed, and his pants around his ankles.

"I should have never met you tonight. I love Troy, Randy." I snatched my dress off the floor, quickly putting it on, and stuffed my bra and panties into my clutch.

"Yeah, right!" Randy snickered. "We'll see what your boy thinks of you now!"

"Fuck you and your threats, Randy!" I ran out of his apartment and never looked back.

Chapter 16

Yeah. Right. Whatever

I thought re-creating the other night would help bring back those lost pages. But the sound of waterfalls, and an entire bottle of wine, didn't do a thing. *Are you sure you want to shut down?* the computer asked. "Just shut up, and shut down already!" I pounced hard on the enter key. The phone rang, startling me. I checked the caller ID: "out of area." Was it her? I was not in the mood tonight. If it is, I'm going to let her have it with both barrels.

"Hello!" I snatched the phone up in a fury.

"You fucking bitch! I hate you!" the female caller barked in a drab French accent.

"I'll kick your ass!" I said with my *Bed-Sty-do-or-die* Mafioso tough-girl attitude. She hung up. I collapsed on the sofa, staring at the phone. I was angry and there was nothing I could do.

I shook my head in disgust. Screw this! As soon as Michael walks through that door, I'm going to confront him.

I heard Michael closing the front door. I stepped into the hall. "Michael, are you cheating on me?" I came right out with it.

Michael started to laugh and headed for the laundry room.

"I'm talking to you! Don't you dare walk away from me!" My voice was loud and full of contempt. He knew better than to take another step. "And I don't see a damn thing funny!"

Michael turned around, looked at me, staring me in the eye. "You're right, I didn't mean to laugh. It's just what you said is so ridiculous."

"I'll tell you what's so ridiculous, a woman who keeps calling my damn house and hanging up in my face! Who is the bitch, Michael?"

"What is this really all about, Charlie? Wedding jitters? Your not being able to write your script? And, please don't say my kids. You knew my situation from the get-go, so don't give me that shit!" Michael paced the floor, getting more defensive by the minute. "You know you got a lot of fucking nerve accusing me. I work hard every day to make sure you don't want for nothing. And all I ask from you is a clean house and a hot meal. I mean damn, how many brothers do you know that would continue to support this dream of yours?" Michael realized what he'd said but it was too late to take it back.

"Don't try to flip the script! Just answer my fucking question or I swear I will tear this house apart!" I was enraged and started to tremble. I think I scared him. He took a deep breath before speaking.

"Damn it, I didn't want to tell you like this."

Michael tried to step toward me but my body language told him that if he wanted to keep his head attached to his body he'd better stand still. "Look, I have an investor, who happens to be a woman. A very wealthy woman, but it's not what you think. She's well connected and is only interested in making money. That's all." Michael looked at me as if he'd been wounded.

"Please! Do I look like a fool to you? There's a woman who's been calling here for weeks. If what you're saying is true, and it's all about business, then why in the hell is she hanging up, and calling me out of my name?! Doesn't she know you have a fiancée!" I screamed.

"Charlie, this is crazy! Anyone could be making these crank calls. What about Juanita?" Michael said, now taking baby steps toward me.

"So tell me, is this investor woman of yours French?" I asked, throwing him off.

"I think so. Yes, actually she is," Michael said, acting like he was unsure.

"Well, it ain't Juanita! You're lying, Michael!" I belted out.

"I'm not lying! Charlie, I may have lied about some of

my double shifts, but I did it because I wanted to surprise you," Michael said, reaching his hand out to me. "Charlie, please, I'm telling you the truth. My investor's name is Natasha and she's an older woman with lots of cash. She's what they call a venture capitalist."

Michael started talking fast as he took me by the hand and pulled me close. "The woman is making my dream, *our* dream come true. I thought you wanted this for me, for us. You know I've always wanted to start my own construction business. If all goes well, I could be signing a lease right before the wedding."

Part of me really wanted to believe him, but my anger had me convinced he wasn't capable of telling me the truth.

"I'm telling you, baby, it's not what you think. I love *you* and I'm going to marry *you*. Why in the world would I jeopardize that?" Michael pleaded.

My mind was pounding with uncertainty. I pulled away, stormed into the bedroom, and slammed the door behind me.

"Yeah, right, whatever!" was all I could say.

Chapter 17

Come Again?

I walked out of Robert's office invigorated. He had approved the pilot script for Alix's show. Once I get the pilot shot, I'm going to spring it on Robert that I want to jump into the producer's ring. Just then Robert called out.

"Lindsay! The writer did a great job on the final draft."

I stopped, and he caught up.

"Obviously you're feeling better?"

"Yeah, it was just a bug," I answered, praying we wouldn't have to relive my near breakdown.

"Just make sure you stay healthy. This show's

going to be incredible. I need you feeling a hundred per-cent from here on out." Robert gave me a reassuring look.

Three o'clock rolled around and the words on my computer screen began to run together. I kept thinking about Troy and Randy. How could I have allowed "it" to happen with Randy? I was branded with my very own scarlet letter. I never wanted to speak about it, think about it, or bring it up again. Suddenly, my line lit up.

"Lindsay Bradley," I answered.

There was a long pause.

"Hello?"

"Lindsay, I need to see you. I know it's late, but have you had lunch yet?" It was Troy. I was elated, oblivious to his strained tone.

"I've eaten already, but I can get off early to meet you." I made myself instantly forget that Troy hadn't called in weeks. For him to ask me to leave the office, it had to be important. I hung up, and quickly wrapped up for the day.

We had been sitting at the Empire Diner for over twenty minutes. Troy barely hugged me when I arrived, and I watched him eat his entire meal practically in silence. I was stuck on weird, and the Empire's cold metal-and-chrome décor, and the hard leather seats, made me even more uncomfortable.

I was about to bite my nail when Troy reached over and pushed my hand away from my face. His familiar touch lightened the mood and I felt better.

We exited Empire. Troy's hand was on the small of my back. I inhaled deeply. It was good to have him back. He stopped midstride and turned to me, lifting my face in his hands. I braced myself. He was finally ready to say the long-awaited words. I pictured myself standing in his kitchen telling him I loved him. Now I was going to finally hear it from him.

"I felt myself falling in love with you a long time ago, Lindsay." My heart danced with delight. If only he would just hurry and tell me now. Troy's words flowed with ease: "But I discovered you aren't the one for me."

"What are you saying, Troy? Where is this coming from?"

He cleared his throat and tilted his head. The sun hit his eyes and they sparkled something devilish. "Look, Lindsay, we can stop the games."

"What games? What are you talking about?" I was dazed.

"I know you slept with Randy."

The earth dropped from beneath my feet. Troy had found out about it. The "it" I vowed to forget. He was trying to be calm, but his anger hung from the edge of his tongue like an icicle.

"You know you really hurt me. I trusted you, but now I'm done. We're done, Lindsay."

I felt as if my body had cracked into a million pieces.

"Hold on . . . please, no, not like this. You don't understand. Please, Troy." I tried to explain, but couldn't. My tongue swelled up. I was fighting back tears. Troy touched my hand. I was numb.

"There's someone else I should've pursued a long time ago, but I got sidetracked with you." He let go of my hand. As angry as I was, pride wouldn't let me cry. My heart pounded faster and faster. I looked up. A taxi was headed toward us. "By the way, Randy was right. Your intentions were always impure. He told me from the beginning it wasn't going to work out," Troy said, flagging the taxi.

Troy opened the door and I grabbed his arm, making a last-minute, desperate plea.

"Randy's full of shit, Troy! He told me the same thing about you! Don't you see, Randy wants what we have. Please just let me explain," I stammered.

"You're the one who's full of it. When you told me you loved me, I admit I didn't know how to handle it. I went to my boy for advice. He said that you did the same thing with him. I wanted to prove him wrong, so I told him to test you. Test what we had. You failed." Troy started to laugh. "All this time I was so worried about you and your boss. I never thought it would be Randy. Damn, some bitches don't have any self-control." Troy served me one too many low blows. I was fed up.

"To hell with you, Troy! Randy told me you've been screwing Robin and everything else with two legs! Yeah, your boy Randy told me all about it. So don't give me a holier-than-thou speech!"

Troy couldn't believe his boy had ratted him out. His face puffed up with anger. "Hear me loud and clear, I'm never going to let a bitch come between me and my boy," and with that he got into the cab and disappeared.

I felt my chest cave in. He had called me a bitch twice in several minutes. The world circled around my head. My legs felt like Jell-O. I don't know how I did it, but I raised my hand and hailed another cab. I slid in and miraculously got out one word, "Uptown."

The smell of curry and Middle Eastern spices filled the backseat. Then Eartha Kitt's famous growl reminding New

Yorkers to "Grrrr! Buckle up!" pierced through the rear speaker. New York cabbies had jumped into the twenty-first century with state-of-the-art celebrity safety messages. However, they were annoying. Listening to one on a good day could drive a sane person insane. So you know what it could do on a day like today!

I felt confined in the cramped backseat, and I was going to lose it for sure if I didn't get out fast. "Stop the cab!" I screamed, banging on the Plexiglas partition with my fist. The taxi had only gotten a block away from the diner. I opened the door as the wheels came to a halt.

"What you doing, crazy lady! You pay!" The driver was going ballistic.

"Pay for what? You didn't take me anywhere!" I screamed. I gave him the very unladylike middle finger, yanked my purse up, and jumped out, but not before scuffing my shoe and ripping my panty hose. The cab driver burned rubber, and flipped me off too.

I started feeling sick to my stomach. Then suddenly, just as I was thinking my guardian angel had failed me, a gypsy cab barreled around the corner of Twenty-third. *Thank you Lord*, I silently mouthed.

I dove into the backseat. No prerecorded corny messages about buckling up from Bernadette Peters, Alan Alda, Joan Rivers, or any other TV, Broadway, or movie star. The cab zoomed up Tenth Avenue.

I couldn't believe all this was coming down on me. It was unfair and Troy wasn't being held accountable for anything. Randy was devious and calculating but I had to give it to him: he played his game well. I never saw it coming. I clasped my hands to keep them from shaking.

Chapter 18

Watch Where
You're Walking

I t's time for Miranda to show me the money! And stop giving me the runaround with these bogus appointments.

I marched right up to her. "Miranda could I please have a minute of your time? It's important."

Miranda looked down at her diamond-studded Rolex. "I'm sorry, Charlie, today isn't good. I'm leaving early, but why don't you set something up with Karen for later in the week."

"Miranda, every time I set a meeting it's canceled. I can't help but feel you're avoiding me," I said, looking her straight in the eyes. Before Miranda could respond Bob, another executive, walked over.

"Miranda, they've changed the location of the meeting. It's now in SoHo. If we're going to be on time we've gotta leave now." Miranda turned to me. "Charlie, trust me, I'm not avoiding you. You and I will sit down soon, promise."

After she hurried off, I looked down at my humble Nine West wristwatch that I'd gotten on sale. I decided I deserved an early day off too. It was high time to spend some quality time with the most important person of all: me.

The revolving doors of the towering office building in which I worked swept me out into the clusters of tourists that Rockefeller Center attracted all year 'round. I quickly high-stepped it past the cacophony of international dialects and chatter. Emerging from the sea of bodies, I finally reached the southern border of Central Park.

I almost forgot how Central Park West stretched for what felt like an eternity. But it was all good. My eyes played from building to building along the skyline that formed a backdrop to the park. Lost in my very own Manhattan rhapsody. Appreciating architectural details along the way was a habit I picked up from Michael.

I figured out two avenues down that I was just around the corner from Michael's site. Spending time with myself is one thing, but the tempting thought of seeing Michael is another. Fact is, I missed him. Maybe I could snag him and treat him to a snack, as a peace-offering, since he was working another double today.

I hate fighting with Michael. He's stubborn and so am I. Since the fight we've barely said two words to each other.

One of us has to back down, and since I'm the one plan-ning our wedding it might as well be me. We have entirely too much at stake. Not to mention I'm horny!

In no time I'd made it to Michael's site. I saw his boys, who had been over to the house for dinner many times. I'm get-ting all hot and bothered just thinking about seeing my man all sweaty in his construction gear.

"Hey guys," I said, waving to the group of workers and looking around for Michael.

"Charlie, long time no see. How are you?" Phillip, one of Michael's oldest buddies, was short with a potbelly. He stood out next to the other workers' buff bodies.

"I'm fine, how's Kathy and the kids?" I asked, as my eyes searched the area.

"She's fine. I'll tell her that you asked about her. You're not looking for Michael, are you?"

"That's exactly what I'm doing. Is he on break?"

"Charlie, he's not here. I think he took the rest of the day off." Phillip looked uncomfortable; he wasn't a good liar.

Michael was busted.

"Oh yeah, that's right. How could I forget. Okay sweetie, listen, you and Kathy have to come by for dinner soon," I said, covering up my anger.

"You got it!" Philip couldn't get away from me fast enough.

I couldn't wait to get to the nearest pay phone. I had a cell, but unlike *her,* I'm not dumb enough to actually call from my own phone. I pulled out the piece of paper that I'd been keeping in my wallet. As I punched in the numbers, I could hear my heart beat. After two rings she picked up, laughing. It was one of those stop-playing-you-know-I'm-ticklish laughs.

"Hello?" It was her all right! I would recognize that damn French accent anywhere. "Hello?" she repeated. I hung up and was ready to vomit.

My gut was telling me that Michael hadn't been working double shifts like he claimed. Instead, he was off tickling some French hoochie. I bet she knew it was me calling and wanted to make sure I heard what a grand old time she was having with my man. That bitch!

After several blocks of me cursing Michael for all he was worth, I needed to stop and take a break. The cute pair of shoes I had on were definitely not made for walking. Thank God there was a restaurant across the street from where I was standing. I peeked in to see what the crowd was like, and one glimpse of the hard-body bartender was enough to convince me. The Shark Bar was definitely a good rest stop.

How do I look? I thought, giving myself the once-over. I was wearing a slim skirt that complimented my odd body type—top heavy, slim waist and small buttocks. I always hated that as a sista I didn't have that infamous "onion." Ya know, a booty so robust that it could make men cry. I gave myself a little pep talk and traipsed my butt right into the Shark Bar.

Taking a seat at the bar, I got the best view of the bartender. It was going to be nice having this handsome male specimen all to myself. I felt like getting into a little trouble.

"Hello sexy, my name is Charlie. Can I have a Midori sour," I said, giving up my best come-hither look.

"Well, hello Charlie, I'm Stevie, I'll be right with you," Stevie returned, with an infectious smile. His smile had me wishing he'd jump right over the counter and take me. I was enjoying being bad today.

Stevie's serious concentration while preparing my drink reminded me of a pharmacist: the way he carefully measured and added each ingredient into the tall glass. His clothes weren't tight fitting, but the curves and cuts of his body were still apparent. I wondered if he was devoted to a woman just as much as he was to the gym?

"Thank you, handsome." I was really feeling myself today, as Kyle would say.

"That smile of yours is irresistible, Miss Charlie. And you've got those big eyes. They kind of remind me of Diana Ross's smoldering sophistication in *Mahogany*."

Stevie was giving me a taste of my own medicine. I was blushing all over and didn't even have a comeback.

"Lucky man, whoever he is," Stevie said, tapping my furnished hand. Yep, he was definitely messing with me now. I looked at my ring, wishing I had the courage to throw it and Michael away.

"My treat," Stevie said, winking at me. It was good to know that if I decided to leave Michael and get back into the singles game . . . I could still play.

Chapter 19

The Meeting

Once the gypsy cab hit the Fifties I jumped out. In the aftershock of Troy breaking up with me, I needed to walk. Twenty blocks later I was exhausted. I decided to stop at an herbal tea store to get some St. John's Wort for my nerves. The sign simply read: Chinese Teas and Herbal Healing.

I entered the store, and a tiny Asian man rushed to greet me.

"What can I do for you?" he asked with a heavy accent.

After he handed me my package of tea, I

noticed a display advertising natural alternatives to medical treatments. "Do you have any teas or herbs for multiple sclerosis?" I wanted to send Faith a care package to let her know I was thinking about her.

"I have just the right tea for you," he said, disappearing behind the curtain that separated the store from the stockroom.

When he returned, he handed me a small brown bag filled with a special tea. I also grabbed a pamphlet from the tea-maker, Hanna's Herbals, in case Faith ever wanted to order directly from them. I handed him the money and thanked him as I exited and continued on my way.

The Shark Bar was only one more block away, at Seventy-fourth and Amsterdam. It was a terrible contradiction, after my stop at the herbal store, but I need a drink, bad!

The bartender, Stevie, was great, and he made a mean Cosmopolitan. My drink, the drink of all drinks. Stevie was Puerto Rican and fine. Sexy and bald with a wild tiger tat on his left shoulder, and cut. His six-foot stature had him looking like a model fresh out of a Dolce & Gabbana ad. The cool thing about Stevie was how down to earth he was. He had a great sense of humor, and he didn't get in your business like most bartenders. He just focused on making a good drink that got you super drunk, but he would crack on you if you skimped on a tip.

I hadn't seen Stevie in a while. Seeing him would be a thrill and my mouth was watering. I could taste his Cosmo walking in the door. The dinner crowd hadn't arrived yet. A soft stool at the bar provided a welcoming remedy.

Stevie had his back turned, mixing a drink and shaking

his tight, perfect butt to the lively music that pumped through the speakers. I leaned into the bar.

"Hey, cutie, do fries go with that shake?"

Stevie recognized my voice immediately. "What's up, luv! Long time, no see."

We hugged and my nostrils welcomed Stevie's crisp Bulgari scent. I felt the weight of somebody's eyes from a few stools down. I cocked my head back to scrutinize a Bohemian type I'd caught giving me the once-over when I walked in. I looked at her wild naturally curly red Afro. She was attractive, but in an eccentric, almost exotic kind of way, brown-skinned with freckles. Where in the world is she from?

"Stevie, let me get a—" I said, swaying to the beat of the music but still distracted by the woman. Stevie cut me off.

"Cosmo straight up! You know I know how you do." Stevie hit the volume and Aretha's "Look into Your Heart" kicked in louder.

I took a long sip of my cocktail. That song epitomized my life and love life right about now. Although my experience outweighed my thirty years on earth, I was living testimony to Madame Ree Ree's message, especially after today.

"Whatever you wanna do, I wanna do it with you, baby, ooh, ooh!" The woman on the other barstool blurted out a verse.

I was intrigued even more by her wacky outburst. Stevie and I looked at each other. I know we were thinking the same thing—*only in New York*. I shook my head. By the way, she was wiggling. She was definitely a free spirit.

"You go girl!" I chuckled, along with Stevie.

Now most people would be completely embarrassed, but not this woman.

"That's right, that's the queen keepin' it real."

She leaned in closer and extended her hand, speaking in a warm direct tone. "Hi, Charlie Thornton. I'm speaking 'cause I feel like it. I'm *not* hitting on you."

I laughed. Sista girl was a piece of work, and out of her mind for sure. I couldn't stop laughing as I returned the gesture, shaking Charlie's hand firmly.

"Lindsay Bradley, and don't even get it twisted!" I retorted. The ice was broken.

"I just happened to be walking by, needed a drink, and this place caught my eye." Charlie smirked at her hidden pun, winking and gesturing toward Stevie. I gave the I'm-with-you-girlfriend nod and took a sip of my Cosmo. Her private joke was all over my radar.

"Well, this is the absolute worst day of my life. My man just dumped me!" My eyes got watery. Charlie passed me a napkin.

"I feel you. My man's in the doghouse now!"

"But I told him I loved him and then he quit me on the street! And then had the nerve to tell me he wanted somebody else."

"Oh, that's cold! Men are selfish, cheating dogs," my new friend fervently stated.

"That's all right, he'll be the one missing out. I hope he has a shitty life. Jerk!"

"Well I say, good riddance! At least you're not like me. I live with my man, and still have to go home to his tired ass."

We toasted and burst into laughter.

"That man had me so mad . . . I was fixin' to put my foot up his—"

"You must be from the South?" Charlie interrupted.

"Sort of. The Midwest. St. Louis. My accent tends to come out when I get mad."

"Ooh, I heard that place is country. They even still wear Jheri curls."

Although I hadn't been back home in years, I felt the need to defend my turf. I looked Charlie up and down. From what I saw, she didn't exactly scream New York City.

"Hold up! St. Louis is a good place to grow up. Church-going people and solid family beliefs. I'll admit some folks *are* stuck in a time warp, but I think that's part of its charm. The question is, what part of Jersey do *you* hail from, because I know you aren't from around here," I said matter-of-factly.

"First of all, I'm from the N.Y." Charlie took a sip of her drink.

"But are you from the N.Y.C.?" I asked, calling her out.

"Another drink, please?" Charlie summoned Stevie.

Aha! I could tell by how she blew me off and began fiddling with her cocktail napkin, she knew I was calling her out. She was busted. I motioned for Stevie to hold up a second.

"Hey, if you're from the great N.Y.C., the next round's on me, but if not, the next two are on you." I nailed her good. "And I'll even be kind and throw in the surrounding boroughs."

Charlie threw her hands up in a surrendering gesture

and confessed. "Okay, okay, Buffalo is my hometown, but it still counts as the great N.Y." We laughed. "Big deal, you got me," she said, downing her drink.

"No, you got me. I feel like being a nice person today. I'll only hold you to one round," I said, sliding my empty glass away. I noticed what Charlie was drinking, and leaned into her. "Look, another piece of advice: Midori sours go right with the concept of the 'Big Eighties,' those Jheri curls you were bagging on, and hoochie mamas. So let me hip you to the new millennium, it's called a Cosmopolitan."

"A what?" she asked.

"It's a martini," I coolly replied, ordering a round.

Watching Stevie closely, I was entranced. My eyes followed the silver shaker. It gleamed off the orange-red spotlight from the overhead lighting. The room seemed still, frozen. The shaker rotated rhythmically, up and down, side to side like it was hovering in midair. The pink liquid flowed effortlessly into each chilled martini glass.

Stevie ran lemon rind around the rim of each glass and dropped it in. He sauntered over and slid our drinks across the bar without spilling a drop. Charlie was caught in a trance too. We both did a double take, looking at each other, then at Stevie, then back to each other.

"Damn!" fell out of our mouths in a syncopated stammer.

Charlie leaned sideways and whispered, "Is this man good looking or what?"

"Stevie is a finger-licking-good Butter Rican Pecan," I said, returning her sentiment.

We gave Stevie a full-body once-over. Charlie elbowed me when Stevie caught the two of us gawking and laughing. He could see we were having too much fun at his expense.

"Looks like my Cosmopolitans have sparked a new friendship."

"I think so," I agreed.

"Definitely!" Charlie backed my play.

I pulled out a business card, jotting down my home and cell numbers. Charlie did the same.

"Hey, St. Louis, I really had a nice time. I only have one good friend, Kyle, and he's a guy. But you're cool. For a country girl." We laughed again.

"Same here, Buffalo girl."

Charlie suggested we meet every Friday after work, which would allow us time to nurse our hangovers on Saturday.

"To living!" She raised her glass.

"To talking to strangers!" I added.

We toasted.

Chapter 20

Cosmos and Conversations

I was glad Lindsay didn't flake out. When she called to confirm the time for our first official "Girls' Night Out," I was shocked. Meeting and exchanging numbers was the "industry thing" to do, but following up was rare. I opened the door to the Shark Bar and Lindsay was busy typing away on her two-way. She looked stressed.

"Hey, girlfriend!" I greeted. Lindsay's phone was ringing off the hook. I looked at her oddly. "Aren't you going to answer that?"

"Nope, I know who it is."

"You got it like that to be dissing a brotha's calls?" I asked.

"Please, I wish. It's my boss, and I'm just not in the mood to talk."

"Then I suggest turning it off. It's Friday and you look like you deserve a breather."

The phone rang again. I observed Lindsay's jumpy body language.

"Hello?" Lindsay paused, stiffening her back. "Yes, Robert." Lindsay stood up abruptly. "Robert you're cutting in and out. I'm sorry, my battery is low." She twisted her mouth and pivoted around listening intently. "Sure, no problem, I'll see you early Monday morning."

I examined her as she hung up the phone. "What was that all about? You look so uptight."

"Mind yours. That only took a minute. Besides, I'm doing as you suggested." She held up the phone. "See, the phone is off!"

"Oh, I see, all right. You're one of those *workaholic* women," I said. Sometimes I think all our electronics are merely fancy balls and chains.

"Please! I am *not* a workaholic!"

"I know one when I see one. Work-a-ho-lic!" I said teasingly.

"What you really ought to be calling me is an *al-co-ho-lic.* 'Cause that's what I'm about to be!" Lindsay joked, anxious to change the subject.

"Well all right! Stevie, let's get this woman a drink!" I said, winking at him.

I was starting to glow from the Cosmo. I had the official "I'm tipsy" glint in my eyes. "So, Miss St. Louis, what made you leave the comforts of your background to join the pack of wolves in N.Y.C.?"

"The harsh realities of not having a chance at a big television career in my hometown. I was way too ambitious for poor pay and limited exposure," Lindsay answered.

"I'm impressed." I really was.

Lindsay raised her drink and winked. "I see myself as a combination of Faye Dunaway's character in *Network* and Oprah Winfrey. I worship that woman." Lindsay's lazy tongue was evidence I wasn't the only one feeling my drink.

"You better work it out, baby FayeFrey!" I raised my glass to her. "Sounds like somebody's sticking to their plans," I said, wishing I could say the same thing about myself.

"We'll see, but what about you, Miss Charlie Thornton?"

Now I had to figure out how to make my nothing sound like something, so I gave it my best shot. "I'm a copywriter for Imagination City, but I'm working on a movie script about the trials and tribulations of four best friends. It's been a struggle because I'm only able to write in the evenings and on weekends." I tried to sound legit.

"Oh, my mother is a writer and she made lots of sacrifices too. But I'm proud to say that after all these years, she is the editor of *Black Writer's Journal*. Her very own poetry quarterly."

"Wait, I've heard of that!"

"Really? Honey, my mother is a character. If it took her until she was a hundred, she was going to see her dream come true." Lindsay took another intoxicating sip of her cocktail. "So what's the rest of your story, Charlie?"

I looked at her strangely. "How much time you got?"

"Plenty," Lindsay said.

"Well, I'll try to make a long story short. I wanted to be a filmmaker. But living in Buffalo there was no way I was going to see that dream come true. Not in a small city like that," I said, happy to see that my cocktail glass was somehow magically refilled. "My passion for writing got the best of me. It was time to make a change, get some courage and step out on faith." I took a tiny sip to refresh.

"I worked two jobs for a whole year, saved my money, and took the next flight here. I was in a New York state of mind," I said dramatically. "My mantra became, 'If I can make it in the Big Apple, I'm the bomb!' " I said, raising my glass once again.

"I heard that. So do you go home often?" Lindsay asked.

"I go back once or twice a year, and for the holidays. Mostly because my granny makes me feel guilty if I don't. That's my girl! Talk about inspiration. She's mine. That woman moved her entire family from the South to Buffalo to pursue her dream of becoming an entrepreneur," I said, putting my glass down. "Granny opened a boutique, record store, and a restaurant. Betty's Texas Red Hots, best known for her famous Betty burgers and old-fashioned milkshakes. Chile, I could kill for one right now!" I said, savoring a time long ago.

"Charlie, sounds like you have all of her ambitious attributes. Look at you, you did the same thing. Left your hometown to go after your dream. I may not know you that well, but from one sista to another, I'm proud of you."

"Thanks, Lindsay. You're all right with me. It feels good to have a black woman being supportive."

Part 2

All Is Fair in Love and War!

Chapter 21

Girlfriends

When Charlie returned from the ladies' room, I had moved from the now crowded bar area to a small corner table. I know she was wondering what the hell was going on. When she left I was fine, now I looked a hot mess. My nose was red and my eyes were swollen.

"Girl, you all right? I wasn't gone *that* long!" Charlie said.

I didn't let her get in her seat good before I hit her with it. "I told you my man broke up with me. But the truth is he did it because he found out I slept with my ex!" My eyes filled up with tears and I fell into Charlie's arms. Poor thing, I could tell she was at a loss, and trying her best to console me. "I'm sorry, you don't even know me that well and I'm hitting you with all my problems," I sniffled.

"No, it's cool. It's just this female bonding thing is very new to me. But it's okay, and your situation isn't so bad," she said, patting my hand lightly.

"You don't have to downplay it. I know it's bad," I said, blowing my nose.

"But you feel crappy enough. I don't need to make matters worse. Listen, if you really love him, don't give up. There's got to be a way to work things out. Men do stuff like this all the time."

I wiped my face and took a deep breath. "There's more."

"I'm listening, but first let's get some more drinks. If you got a skeleton in your closet, best thing to do is clean it out!" Charlie shifted forward, encouraging me.

After two more Cosmos, I had laid it all out.

"This is like a soap opera! Don't you know, girl, there ain't nothing worse than a man who's got his ego on his ass, and the woman he wants dumps him? Sooner or later you were gonna have to deal with this Randy character anyway," Charlie said, pained by my dilemma.

"Yeah, but see, men stick together. It doesn't matter that in the end Troy is the man I love and want to be with." I was getting weaker by the moment. "I just want my relationship back with Troy," I said, burying my face in my hands.

"You may have been wrong, but Troy and Randy did you in." Charlie was charged up. "Chile, sounds like Troy is on a power trip. He had you on a string like a puppet and you didn't even know it! You can't build on a weak foundation," she said, pounding her fist on the table. "He never had any faith in you from the beginning!"

"I feel so bad, Charlie," I said pitifully.

"Don't you sit up here and feel guilty. I smell a rat. Randy played both of y'all." Charlie was fuming. I took a hearty gulp of my Cosmo and swallowed hard. "Honey, if this ain't a bunch of bull, I don't know what is. All Troy did was turn things around on you, so that he could get out of this guilt-free."

I took a napkin and wiped my face, giving Stevie the nod for another round.

Stevie returned with drinks in hand. "Ladies, this is round three. It's on me, and I made them a little weaker. I don't want you two beautiful women getting to a point where you can't handle yourselves."

"More men need to be like you," I said.

Stevie blushed, shaking his head as he walked away.

"I'm not going out like this, Charlie. I'm about to be on a serious mission," I said, licking the alcohol residue from my lips.

"What's your mission, Miss Lindsay?" Charlie asked curiously.

"I'm not sure. I do know this, I've gotta get this monkey off my back and stop being jerked around by men!" I said, fueled by the mixture of the Cosmopolitans and my anger.

"Now, that's what I'm talking about."

"I want to make Troy feel just as bad as I do right now." I looked over at Charlie and I could tell something evil was lurking in both our heads. I know it was in mine.

"So you're talking about revenge?" Charlie grimaced.

"That's right. Payback is a mother!" I said. "The first thing I need is a plan, and I'm sure you can help me come up with a darn good one. We're two smart, attractive women." I pulled out a pen and started scribbling on a napkin. I held it up. "Check it out! Our very own Code of Arms for bringing down the enemy! Listen, number one, *hit him where it hurts!*" I said excitedly.

"I got one! Number two, *celebrate your newfound single status by looking sexy as hell so you can meet a new man!*" Charlie interjected.

"Good one! Then, number three, *create a fabulously scandalous rumor and make the ex jealous!*" I felt revived, as I feverishly kept writing.

"And lastly, number four, *keep it moving, don't look back, and don't let old memories trap you in the sack!*" Charlie added, as I eagerly finished jotting down the Code of Arms and held up the napkin.

We were amped.

"To the Cosmo Code of Arms saving all womankind!" I said, putting my fist out.

"Our future depends on you, girl!" Charlie cheered with drunken enthusiasm, returning the gesture, giving me a rowdy pound.

Chapter 22

More Cosmos and Conversations

To women breaking the rules!" I raised my glass in a firery toast. *Clink!* I tapped Charlie's glass a bit too hard. I appreciated my new friend Charlie helping me get over my heartache.

"So, St. Louis, do you ever miss it?" Charlie said, slurring a bit.

"Miss what?" I replied, lighting the table candle. To no avail, I was zoning in to flickers of Troy.

"Home. Do you go back much?"

"Not as much as I'd like to. Work keeps me too busy. I miss my mother's entertaining, though.

She's always having these soirees at the house with all her famous writer friends."

"Really!" Charlie was intrigued.

"Honey, I know you're not going to believe it, but James Baldwin, Margaret Walker, and Gwendolyn Brooks all made our house a pit stop. Good food and spiritual nourishment. Everybody knew Mama could put her foot in some Creole gumbo."

"Forget the food. I would've killed for all that history," Charlie said.

"Yeah, but you haven't tasted her gumbo! Since I've been living here the *Zagat* guide has become my second mother."

We ordered another round of Cosmopolitans. It was Charlie's turn to toast.

"To living!"

I remembered she had said that when we first met. I needed to get to the bottom of what Miss Charlie meant. From the looks of her hand, she *was* living to me. Certainly living the "Lindsay American Dream" with a 2.5 carat ring sitting on her finger. I was dying to know . . .

"So Charlie, what's up with that big fat rock on your finger?" And a rock it was. Clear, flawless, pristine.

"Oh, this?" she said, cracking a smile and holding up her hand. "Just a little engagement bling bling."

"How'd you do it? It seems like half the men are in jail and the other half are gay. I can't figure it out. Men say they want a woman who has it going on. So you get it going on, and they go for the chicks with no aspirations."

"You know what your problem is, Lindsay? You spend

too much time worrying about a man. You know how I got mine? By not worrying about one."

"So it's that simple?" I couldn't imagine.

"Men always want what they can't have. And with my fiancé Michael, I wasn't pressed. But I will admit, sometimes I envy single women. I miss the sport of hunting men." Charlie winked.

"The hunt gets boring. At least you have a man sleeping in your bed every night."

"Yeah, you do have a point, because my man does know how to put it on me." Charlie fanned herself slowly while sipping her Cosmo.

"It's all that, huh?"

"All that and then some!" Charlie dramatically swatted me on my shoulder.

"Girl, does he have any brothers?" I laughed.

"Girl, please, I didn't say he was perfect."

"Well, you've snagged one, so you clearly have them pegged," I said, taking a sip from my glass.

"Nah, I'm just a pimpstress when it comes to men."

"A pimpstress?" I was amused.

"I'm a pimp without all the stress."

Charlie was trying her best to look serious. I had to do everything I could to keep from spitting out my drink. I swallowed hard, triggering us both to crack up.

"Please!" I rolled my eyes.

"You wish, softy!" Charlie hiccuped.

"I hope you do know something about men. 'Cause I can't figure them out to save my life!" We both let out rowdy belly laughs. "*Big*-talking Buffalo girl can't handle her drink, acting just like an amateur. I should have never turned you on to Cosmos because now you're spacing out. A pimpstress, whoever heard of such!" I teased, calling Charlie out as the laughter died.

"Girl, the pimpstress is retiring come this Christmas Eve. Even though I still haven't found my wedding dress."

"That's a shame. You're way off schedule. Where's your wedding planner?" I asked.

"You're looking at her!" Charlie frowned.

"Okay, that's it! I'm officially your unofficial maid of honor and we are going to get that dress!"

"Cool! Now that we've gotten that settled, let's get back to the mission at hand," Charlie said mischievously.

"Damn I just got a bad taste in my mouth thinking about Randy, and about Troy and Robin gallivanting around town."

"Don't let Troy and that girl sidetrack you. The way to feel victorious is to attack what Troy cherishes most."

"That's easy. Money, women, and his ego."

"Hmm, we've got lots to work with," Charlie said.

"We sure do," I said, as we gave each other sly grins.

We exited the bar . . .

"Are you sure you don't want to share a taxi?" I asked.

"We're going in opposite directions. Thanks anyway. I'll be fine."

"Okay, get home safe and I'll see you next week. And don't worry, I've got your wedding dress covered!"

"Bet!" Charlie gave a playful salute.

Our first mission was in place. I hailed a cab heading up-town, and Charlie headed for the downtown train. It had been a long time since I bonded with a sister who wasn't blood related and since I actually laughed aloud. Tara, Judy, and I spent more time gossiping, talking about the latest sample sales, and driving ourselves nutty with work. Hanging with Charlie was just basic fun.

Maybe something was missing with me and my crew? Maybe partaking in life's simple offerings—good conversation and laughter—was fueling my fascination with this new wild-haired, freckle-faced woman who had the arrogance of a man. Whatever it was, I was excited and wanted to know more about Charlie. Something told me the two of us together couldn't be anything but trouble.

Chapter 23

Extra! Extra!

Rule Number 1: Hit him where it hurts!

I blew into the Shark Bar carrying an armload of newspapers and magazines. I was wearing my *Ab Fab*–inspired, papergirl outfit, complete with a Lola newsboy cap, vintage Marc Jacobs jean blazer and knickers, and Gucci pumps.

"Vavavavoom!" Charlie said, checking out my outfit.

"I dressed for the occasion." I spun around quickly. "Follow me," I said, leading her to a small corner table.

"Check it out! Hot off the presses," I said, dropping the stack of papers on the table and sitting down next to her. Charlie picked up *Time Out New York*. "Feast your eyes on page 182, loverboy himself." I pointed.

Charlie opened up the magazine. "He may be a dog, but he's a cute dog," she said, referring to the picture of Troy that was smack in the middle of the personals. Her eyes went wide as she started to read. " 'Age, thirty-one, occupation, porn video director; looking for sensitive bookworm type who likes to get freaky and loves show tunes; weight no problem, the bigger the better.' " She paused, looking at me in amazement, then continued reading. " 'My favorite on-screen sex scene: any scene featuring multiple men having sex in the underground hit *Off Da Hook I* and *II*. I also loved the kissing scene in *Kiss Me Guido*.' "

"Bam!" I said, taking out the *Village Voice* personals and hitting her with another.

" 'Need a spanking? Video director, 31, will put you over his knee and spank your bare butt; good with first-timers, and seeks overweight guys 18 to 35 years old. Call Troy Barnes, 917–555–2828 or work 212–555–7000.' " Charlie's eyes got even bigger. "Girl, you are bad, bad, bad!"

"Oh, but I'm *so* good! But wait, there's more," I said, pulling out *Newsday*, and signaling to Stevie that we were finally ready for a round of Cosmos.

" 'Private pleasures, hot erotic fantasies. Introducing Gay Bachelor-Grams by Troy Barnes, 917–555–2828.' Ooh, girl, I bet Troy's phone is ringing off the hook. The *chub club* is loving him!" Charlie said, relieving Stevie of the glasses.

"To a successful mission!"

"I'll drink to that!" Charlie sealed the toast with a gentle tap. "Troy is going to flip out when he gets wind of this, Lindsay."

"Oh, I know, that's why I took out so many ads. I wanted to make sure I didn't miss any," I said, trying to imagine the look on Troy's face when he found out. "That's what he gets for messing with Lindsay Bradley! Cosmo rule number one, hit him where it hurts, ain't no joke!"

"And we've only just begun," Charlie added with a raised eyebrow. "Time to start on your next mission," she announced. "You need to get your groove back pronto!"

"Girl, you don't have to tell me twice. I'm ready to get sexy as hell!" I said.

"Meet a man . . ." she hinted.

"And make Troy jealous!" we exclaimed. We were out of control.

"I've got just the place too! Shake D's multiplatinum party. It's going to be hot!" I said, smiling.

"You mean Shake the rapper-producer?" Charlie's eyes went wide.

"That's him! And I'm gonna go for it! Mr. Troy hates his guts. Shake jerked him on a video he was supposed to shoot for one of his artists a while ago."

Charlie's face lit up. "Brilliant! What better man to get than Shake. Hello, rule number two!" Charlie said as she spun around with her eyes closed and started humming and swishing her body side to side.

Chapter 24

Hot Sex on a Platter

Rule Number 2: Celebrate your newfound
single status by looking sexy as hell
so you can meet a new man!

I paced the living room, cramming my survival kit essentials into my purse: Mac lip glass, lip liner, credit cards, and my driver's license.

"You better hurry up. Shake's parties are infamous for filling up quickly and then you can't get in. We have to leave in five," I screamed out to Charlie, who was in the bathroom. I had suggested that Charlie get dressed at my place since she had been arguing with Michael a lot lately. It was fun to have girls' night. "Oh, you trying to hurt some-body tonight, huh?" I joked.

"I hope so."

"Don't let me have to tell Michael on you."

"You gotta find him to tell him. It's not like he cares anyway," Charlie snapped.

"What's going on?"

"Michael's been pulling a lot of overtime lately but I haven't seen an increase in our joint checking account. Who knows what he's really doing, but girl, don't mind me. I'm not about to put a damper on our night," Charlie said. I could tell she needed some cheering up.

"Well, the way you're looking tonight, Michael better get his ass home before some other man beats him to it."

"This ring does come off!" Charlie said, waving her hand in the air.

"Please! You're always bragging about your fine-ass man, and how he puts it on you. Honey, you ain't going no where. So shut it up!"

We laughed.

"Well, all I know is the men are going to be all over you tonight. Girl, you're looking too hot!" Charlie said.

"I'm wearing my rent again," I joked. "But it feels great to look fierce!"

Outside Lot 61 was a zoo. The bouncers, big, tough, and mean dressed in black Goth, surrounded the main door-man, Mercedes, an outrageously dressed drag queen, wear-ing a long black dress and an ostrich-fur leather coat, complete with a fire-red pageboy wig. Miss Mercedes held up the red velvet rope, screeching out commands.

"No, not you! Not her! Yes him and you, but not them!"

I'd never waited outside a club before and I wasn't about to tonight. I yanked Charlie by the hand and we bum-rushed our way to the front of the line. I recognized Big Mike, a bouncer from Lotus, and he cleared a path for us. Miss Mercedes gave us a catty glance.

Once inside, we got into the flow right away and ordered two Cosmos. Lights bounced off the walls, floors, and ceiling at hyper-speed.

A slew of hip-hop's royalty was in the house, Missy Elliot, Queen Latifah, LL Cool J, and Usher.

"I'm glad we came out tonight, Charlie."

"Me too. Nothing will make Troy happier than knowing you're lying in bed crying your eyeballs out. Part of feeling good is moving on, and there are lots of hotties to choose from in here." Charlie gave an exhausted smirk before sipping her Cosmo.

"You're right, but look at Troy. Why is it that a guy can start over so quickly, move on to the next, as if the relationship meant nothing?"

"That's because men don't think of sex the way we do. We get so caught up in the emotional part of it that we don't even enjoy it for what it is. Pleasure, pure and simple. We have to learn to do what they do. Wham! Bam! Thank you *man*!" Charlie jeered, and we slapped five.

Charlie noticed a tall brown-skinned guy across the room dressed in a tailor-made suit, wearing lots of diamonds and platinum. "Check it! Twelve o'clock. Mr. Show-Stopper himself. I see why he's the perfect carrot to dangle in front of Troy's face."

I looked in the direction she was pointing in and saw

Shake, who was berating a group of waiters for mixing up his order. A bevy of models flanked his side.

"Oh no, I changed my mind."

"No way! We didn't come all the way here for you to chicken out."

"Do you see all those gorgeous women with him?"

"And? Look at you! You look amazing. You better get over there and get that!" Charlie gave me a shove.

"This is insane! I've changed my mind, he's got four kids by three different mamas, and I heard he's a major power freak." I continued to run down Shake's bio to Charlie.

"Lindsay, who cares? You're on a mission!"

I'd known Shake for years. Back in the day he was just plain old Fredrick Davis. I suddenly remembered why I never went out with him. He was arrogant then, and ain't no new money or records gonna change that—fame no doubt made him worse. "I will not have him dissing me." I nonchalantly took another sip from my drink.

"Fine. I understand that you're scared. I guess Troy will just continue to think that you're a loser and he'll keep walking over women like they're doormats." Charlie was pushing all the right buttons. I was a fool once, but not twice. I caught her drift and tossed out a sneaky look.

"Well, it *has* been a while. Might be nice to say hi."

"A brotha like Shake would definitely put Troy to shame," Charlie encouraged.

A waiter floated by with Lemon Drop shots. Charlie and I grabbed a couple on the way, collecting a bit of liquid courage.

Shake welcomed me with open arms. "What's up, Lindsay! You look incredible." Shake gave me an extra long hug.

"Thanks, and congrats on all your success."

"It would be better if I had someone to share it with," Shake whispered back, attempting to nibble on my ear. He was up to his old tricks.

Shake popped a bottle, and we got lost in the madness of hot beats and smoky air. Shake's power and fame was suddenly becoming very enticing.

Two bottles later, Shake signaled for his driver to make moves.

Charlie's night had ended. She was now safe and sound in her bed, but mine was just beginning.

I was tuned in to the deep hum of the Bentley as it zoomed back across the Manhattan Bridge from Brooklyn. Prickly heat surged over my skin and I felt tingly. The champagne was in full effect. I giggled out loud at my naughty thought of stripping down to my birthday suit. The straps of my lace and satin tank hung off my shoulders. I leaned my head back against the headrest. My eyes followed the blurred lights of Canal Street into the Holland Tunnel.

Shake kissed my lips, moving down across my breasts. His mouth and tongue sought refuge in between my legs. His mouth camped out for about thirty minutes and I don't know how many orgasms I had. By the time I figured it out, we were pulling up in front of his sprawling New Jersey estate.

I woke up the next morning hung over, with a screaming headache but gushing with delight. I had to double-take the muscular, mocha limbs peeking from beneath the crisp white sheets. It was Shake. My eyes surveyed the room. Whew! I was relieved to see the wrapper and used condom on the nightstand. Thank you Lord! I sunk into the covers. My eyes sparked with menace: mission accomplished.

Chapter 25

Lovely Day

Lindsay planned for us to go uptown to the Mirror Image, to get our hair done by the Dominican sistas.

"What time is our appointment?" I asked.

"We don't have one!" Lindsay said, hopping into the car.

Lindsay sharply whipped into the perfect spot on 108th and Columbus, right in front of the hair salon.

We opened the door to energetic salsa. About ten operators were lined up on both sides of the shop with standard barber chair setups to service their customers. Some were getting streaked or permed and others the famous wash and set. Marilyn, the stout cashier, spotted Lindsay. She quickly put her bowl of arroz con pollo down and rushed over to hug Lindsay.

"Hola, mami!" Marilyn exclaimed.

"Hola, Marilyn! Cómo está?" Lindsay replied, going toe to toe.

"Muy bien, y tu?" Marilyn replied, licking her greasy fingers before wiping them on a tissue stuffed in her pants pocket.

"Bien, mami, bien!" Lindsay continued to impress me.

"Heifer, you speak Spanish?" I nudged her hard.

"I speak a little somethin' somethin'. Hello! These are my peeps!" Lindsay said, with smoldering bravado, turning back to Marilyn.

"Marilyn, this is *mi amiga. Dos* wash *y* sets," Lindsay continued as her Spanish began to waver.

I nudged Lindsay again and leaned in. "Hold up, miss. Wash *y* set! You can't hardly speak Spanish." I cracked up.

"Look, I'm in my element. Don't hate the player . . ."

"Yeah, yeah, hate the game. Old tired sayin'!" I said, shaking my head. She almost had me.

Within ten minutes we were under the sink. *"Mira mamis"* and *"aquí aquís"* flew over our heads. For the first time, with Lindsay's encouragement, I was going to let go of my tight, curly afro. The fact that Lindsay promised there would be no chemicals eased my fear, and I was excited.

We were zoomed to the hair-setting stop, plopped into chairs, while rows of plastic magnetic rollers were slapped on our heads. I did everything to hold in my laughter as I glanced in the mirror and saw how ridiculous Lindsay and I looked.

She handed me a magazine as we got comfortable under the hair dryers. The Home Shopping Network was playing on the overhead television opposite.

"Now look at those hideous dolls," I said, looking up. "What are they?"

"Aw, kissing porcelain leprechauns. You know you want them as a wedding gift," Lindsay teased.

"I would be so damn mad if I opened one of my gift boxes and saw that mess."

"I think they're kinda cute, only twenty-nine ninety-nine, little, lucky symbols of love."

"Yeah, perfect for two lovebirds."

"Lovebirds who want to peck each other to death," Lindsay said, hinting she had something, or someone else, in mind for those dolls.

She started digging in her purse. She pulled out her organizer and cell phone, like she'd just struck oil. She looked back at the TV, quickly dialing the number on the screen, while flipping through the pages of her organizer.

"If you value your life, you'd better not be ordering me those dolls," I said, poking my head out from underneath the dryer.

"Operator, I'd like to order one hundred of the leprechaun porcelain dolls," she said, shushing me and speaking into the phone. "Oh, yes, they *are* beautiful. I collect leprechauns as a hobby. Today is indeed my lucky day," she said with a fake laugh, looking at me with a big shit-eating grin on her face.

Lindsay tore a page out of her organizer and flashed it in front of my eyes. It was Troy's credit card number.

"He gave it to me to order furniture for his new house. As anal as I am, he should know I don't throw important stuff like this away," she said, covering the phone. "Yes, I'll be using my Visa," Lindsay said mischievously, returning to the operator.

"Now, that's cold," I said, loving every devious minute.

Just then, I looked at the television, and the latest George Foreman Grill was on display. "Lindsay, tell her you'll take twenty-five of those," I whispered, jumping in on the action.

By the time our hair had finished drying, a truckload of dolls, enough grills to pass out to the neighborhood, and a large collection of gaudy cubic-zirconia jewelry was on its way to Troy's office. We were still laughing.

"Poor Troy, I might actually start to feel sorry for him soon," I said.

"Not!" we shrieked, giving each other high-fives as we took seats back in front of the mirrors.

Once the rollers were out, I watched out of the corner of my eyes in the mirror as the technicians artfully brushed each section of my hair in constant circular motions. I noticed how with each rhythmic stroke the technician skillfully inserted a jumbo bobby pin, as if laying railroad track.

"Is this how it's supposed to look?" I questioned, peeking over at Lindsay, fearing this was the new style.

"It's called a doobie. Just go with the flow," she said calmly with her eyes closed.

An hour later, the pins were removed. My hair was gorgeous and for only fifteen dollars! I couldn't stop smiling as

I handed over a twenty. Shaking my surprisingly longer hair, which brushed against my shoulders, I exclaimed, "Just call me Miss Jackson!" We strutted out the door as Lindsay called out, "*Gracias, mami*, see chu next week!" She waved good-bye.

"You are somethin', but like I always say, you all right with me," I said, getting into Lindsay's car. "Hope you got a full tank of gas, 'cause we're headed for Brooklyn."

Lindsay's car zoomed down the expressway as the music bumped, Bill Withers singing "Lovely Day." Lindsay and I sang along. Off key and all.

Lindsay and I shuffled down the parade of street vendors along Fulton Street, headed to the Pink Hand Nail Shop.

"Come on, check 'em out. I got FUBU, Sean Jean, Ecko—I give you good price, good price today." The voice belonged to a stocky Jamaican man who yelled out from behind a cluttered booth of Afrocentric hats, purses, and sweatsuits.

"No, thank you," Lindsay said.

As we walked along we saw an older Muslim woman who had set up shop with a table full of old books and incense. Unlike the male vendors, she wasn't pushy. Her calm state was inviting. A small book caught Lindsay's attention.

"I had this as a little girl. *Silver Pennies*, poetry about fairies. Man, I loved this book!" Lindsay held the book close to her chest.

"Then it's yours. Two dollars please." The lady gave a warm smile. Lindsay gladly paid her.

I sifted through a stack and noticed a small tattered paperback. I picked it up. The title was *Stand Up, Speak*

Out, Talk Back! The Key to Assertive Behavior. I handed it to the lady.

"How much is this?" I asked.

"Oh, that's only a dollar," she replied.

"Trust me, it's worth more than you know. I'll take it." I paid the lady, grabbing the poetry book from Lindsay and replacing it with the paperback. I wanted Lindsay to get a good view of the book's title.

"I don't need a guide on how to deal with Robert. I'm very assertive and direct when it comes to him! I'm not intimidated by my boss!"

I shrugged my shoulders and proceeded to the nail shop. "Who are you trying to convince, me or you?"

Lindsay kept reading and rereading the large, bold, red print on the back of the book: "Are you in charge of your own life? Or do other people run it?"

"Whatever! I don't care what you do with your funky little dollar," Lindsay said, sounding like a two-year-old.

"Baby, that dollar was well spent. A true investment!" Lindsay swatted me with the book.

Lindsay and I climbed into the now vacant pedicure stands, and as we perused magazines, enjoying foot massages, I tapped Lindsay. "I can't wait until tonight! Being seen out in public with Shake is going to up the ante!" I said, shaking my hair once again.

"I told Shake about how Troy and I are on the outs."

"I bet he couldn't wait to flaunt you in front of him either." The devil was getting the best of me.

"And he'll get his chance! I know the event coordinator

and she said Troy already RSVP'd. You know that pseudo-cultural Negro's got to be in the house. So the mission is on!"

"Shake is serving his purpose! And you will look like a true star!"

Chapter 26

Fame—All That Glitters Ain't Gold

Rule Number 3: Create a fabulously scandalous rumor and make the ex jealous.

The limo pulled to a slow halt in front of the Obie Gallery in SoHo. I stepped out of the backseat wearing a sexy Catherine Malandrino dress and a pair of strappy Manolo Blahniks. Taking Shake up on his offer to go out in public for our second date was going to cause mayhem in the industry.

Tonight was the opening of a new Gordon Parks exhibition. A small crowd of paparazzi gathered in front and snapped away. I wasn't really planning to be caught on film. The key was never to leave evidence. I tried my best, but there was no way to avoid it.

Shake and I entered the gallery arm in arm and were served champagne immediately. Troy's was one of the first faces we saw. I should've known his high-profiling wanna-be self would be the first on the scene. Troy was enraged as he watched our entrance. Shake was basking in it, and made it a point to walk up to Troy and give him a pound.

Four glasses of champagne later, Shake had me pinned securely to a wall in the far corner of the gallery. However, I was busy scanning the room for Troy. Bull's-eye! I spotted him and we locked eyes. I could see the distaste on his face. I pushed Shake off, excused myself, and headed to the ladies' room.

"Why are you here with him, Lindsay?" Troy said, cutting off my path.

"Why do you care? Shouldn't you be off somewhere with Robin?"

"She has nothing to do with this!"

"She has everything to do with this, Troy!"

I moved past him into the bathroom. Speaking with Troy had made me furious, and I wanted to go home.

After a few minutes I made my way back to Shake. "Hey, I'm sorry, I feel sick. I think I'll just need to head in."

"Word? Okay, boo, let me get my driver and we can bounce."

My feet hurt from my three-inch stiletto heels. Untying my straps, I let my toes sink into the limo's thick plush carpet.

Shake pulled out a bag of weed and told his driver to take the park route, but a late-night Central Park drive was not exactly what I had in mind. Since it seemed like I was stuck with Shake for the moment, when he finished rolling the blunt, I joined him and took a deep hit. About halfway through the park, Shake called out for the driver to pull over. He grabbed me with one arm, pulling me out of the limo, while with his free hand he scooped a bottle of Cristal out of the mini-fridge.

I surveyed a pitch-black Central Park. I was spooked, tiptoeing barefoot through the cold wet grass that stuck to my feet. Shake led me deep into the park.

"See, boo, this is what I'm talking 'bout. I wanna do you everywhere, in the park, lavish hotels, the beaches in the South of France."

"Is that right?" I said flatly as he handed me the last of the blunt. I hit it as fast as I could. I would've taken a handful of narcotics to get through the rest of the night. I'd had just about enough of Shake's slimy-sweet, streetwise rhetoric. I just wanted to tell him to shut up. The mission was getting the best of me.

We'd walked so far I could barely see the Bentley's yellow parking lights. I heard the ripple of water and the full moonlight illuminated the outline of a gazebo. I figured we must be near the boathouse. Shake popped the cork, took a long swig, and started kissing me. I closed my eyes tight and tried to pretend I wasn't there.

"Come on, Shake. It's cold and scary. I heard there are rats in the park too." I was trying my best to be nice. I really wanted to say, *Could we just get this over with already.*

I was bent over, bracing my elbows on my knees.

"You like that? Yeah, yeah! You feel that?" Shake said, spanking my butt.

I couldn't feel anything. The only thing big was his ego. It would've been more enjoyable to submerge myself in a tub of boiling hot water and watch my flesh melt away.

I was repulsed by my own behavior. "Just stop!" I stood up and pushed him away. I was light-headed and slightly disoriented, but I had to get control over the situation. "Shake, take me home!"

"What!"

"You heard what I said! Take me home, now!"

Shake's response was preempted, because suddenly I looked sick.

"Damn, you don't look so good," he said, backing up. "I can't have you throwing up and shit, my suit cost ten g's. This is Versace." I quickly put my hand over my mouth and he rushed me to the car.

I could see my apartment building at the bottom of the hill. Shake was still running off at the mouth, making all sorts of promises.

"Yo, I'm gonna fix you, take you shoppin'. You like Barneys? Bergdorfs? What about Henri Bendel? Yeah, yeah, all that. It's gonna be bananas!"

His hip-hop lingo was making me nauseous again. My head was throbbing. I curled my lips up at him. I didn't need him to take me to Bendel. I could take myself. Didn't this Negro have to go somewhere and pay child support?

The car pulled in front of my building. I thanked him for his kindness. I was being facetious, but he was just too stupid to know it.

Chapter 27

Home

Pastor Harris stood in front of the congregation. His words resonated deeply as he spoke from a book of the New Testament.

"Turn with me, Church, if you will, to Mark 8, verse 36: *'For what will it profit a man if he gains the whole world and loses his own soul'*? Church, say Amen."

"Amen!"

Pastor was building to a close. "Getting caught up in money, material things, our jobs, careers, forgetting about the important things like family . . ."

"Yes Jesus!" Granny shouted.

"You better preach!" I was filled with the spirit.

"Our husbands, our wives, our children, humph, even our own selves!" Pastor continued. "Somebody better praise the Lord!"

As he finished the sermon, the choir began to hum and the organist came in with "I Won't Complain."

"Who's gonna be there for you! God's gonna be there for you!"

"Hallelujah!" Lindsay stood up and began waving her arms in the air. Tears were running down her face. My girl caught the Holy Ghost.

After a great service we headed for Aunt Malinda's house, where my engagement party would be held. Aunt Malinda's house was always family headquarters for big occasions. Out of all the homes in the family, Malinda's house was the favorite. It wasn't the biggest, fanciest, or even the neatest. As a matter of fact, it was downright junky, real country kinfolk stuff, but it was cozy.

As long as I could remember, it was always Malinda and Lonnie. Two odd folks, because my aunt's body was thick like a man. She was full-figured and hairy. She never cared too much for makeup or a comb, but she was a natural beauty in her own way, with a sweet baby face. Uncle was tall and wiry. He was so bony everything he wore was too big and hung off him, but the one perfect thing on him was his half-afro. It was always freshly blown out and shaped.

The family joked that it was a half-afro because in the center of the afro sat a perfect bald spot. It was two or three inches in diameter, like a large doughnut hole. Uncle had a quick tongue and sense of humor just like Richard Pryor. At every family get-together he'd have the whole family dying laughing.

I was very proud of my family. I was getting married, and the only folks I invited were the ones that I loved, trusted, and cared about.

"Hey girl, I just met your uncle and he's a trip!" Lindsay finally came down from her nap. Yep, my girl took off work just for me. She said with her being my "official-unofficial bridesmaid," coming to my dinner was the least she could do. Personally, I think the poor girl's feeling guilty for not helping me find that killer dress. With all our misbehaving, who had time? Lindsay was still carrying around the bride's dress catalog, promising that the next mission was to get my dress.

"Thought I forgot? I'm on it, don't you worry!" Lindsay said, looking around. "So where's this Kyle I've been hearing so much about? I still can't believe, after all this time we've known each other, I haven't met him. Is he still working on that project in L.A.?" Lindsay asked.

"Girl, Kyle is mister jet-setter. He's out in San Francisco now working on a new project for the company. You know he loves it! He missed his last flight. He's been calling all day apologizing. Don't worry, you'll meet him at the wedding."

"Anything I can help with?" Lindsay fit right in with the family.

"No, we got everything covered," my granny said, walking in with a boxload of meat. Granny was aging well, still in good shape with her petite five-foot-five frame. You could see that she had been a knockout back in her day.

And Granny carried on as if she still was. Now she was a grand diva!

I relieved her of the meat and took it out in the backyard. It was my mother's shift on the grill, giving Uncle Lonnie a break. I placed the box of meat down and my mother looked at me and started to cry all over again.

"My baby girl, look at you. I'm so proud." Mama had the biggest set of eyes attached to the tiniest head, now that she was wearing a short blond crop.

I went back inside to check on Michael and his parents. This was the first time both sides were meeting. Michael was a nervous wreck, with things being rocky between us. He knew I'd told Granny everything. I guess he was worried that she would take a switch to him.

I still didn't believe Michael's story about his female investor, but my wedding plans were in motion, and too much time and money had been spent, so I couldn't let my suspicions get in the way. My family was excited about my wedding. But when I walked into the living room, it looked like it was killing Michael's family, the Riveras, to be in each other's company. I'd never seen such reserved folks. They sat on the sofa, all in a row, already dressed for dinner, with their hands neatly folded in their laps.

Veronica, Michael's mother, was beautiful with thick luscious hair, flawless skin, and exotic eyes—I saw now where Michael got his eyes. She looked several years younger than her age, but she dressed in clothes that made her look like a senior citizen. Veronica was cold and emotionless.

"Mrs. Rivera, you look beautiful today," I said as I leaned

over to kiss her on the cheek. Her stiff body language told me that she wasn't familiar with this kind of contact.

"Thank you, Charlie," she dryly replied.

Ricardo, Michael's father, was a submissive man. The only time he raised his voice was to make an apology of some kind, and apologies were all that seemed to come out of his mouth.

"You look great too, Mr. Rivera." I smiled, leaning in to kiss him. He jumped.

"Thanks, Charlie, you too. Sorry, didn't mean to jump like that," he said bashfully before returning his attention to my grandfather, a distinguished man who always kept his natural salt-and-pepper mane intact. Grandpa was entertaining them with his military stories. I glanced at Michael, who was looking pretty hot in all black. He blew me a kiss and gave me a reassuring smile.

Dinner had been a hit and all the guests had had a great time. Only my family was invited to the "after party." Needless to say, the house was packed and the music was jumping. Blackstreet's "Booty Call" filled the room. "Oh my God's" and "Awh, that's my shit!" were heard from everybody in the place. The living room instantly turned into a dance floor courtesy of all the men rearranging the furniture.

Everybody jumped up and started doing the Booty Call, another, jazzier version of the Electric Slide. This kind of dancing was prehistoric in the city clubs. But the song was banging, and I couldn't sit still. I had to learn. I jumped in between my mother and aunt. They were more than eager to teach me the moves.

"Awh, watch out now! Yeah, baby girl, that's it!" Mama did every move so hard and so perfect I thought she was gonna hurt something in the process.

"Break it down! Yeah, she's got it, y'all!" Auntie yelled out as she broke it *all* the way down. Everyone cheered me on, glad to see that I was still one of them. Happy to know the city hadn't changed me. I was still their little Charlie. "Booty Call" was played twice, back to back. Only this time, Lindsay couldn't sit still. She jumped onto the floor.

"The Booty Call ain't nothing but the cha-cha in the Lou—that's St. Louis to y'all," Lindsay said, kicking off her shoes to represent her hometown.

"You go girl!" my family chanted Lindsay on. I could tell my girl was missing her peeps and a trip back home was just what she needed. By the time we stopped, everybody was soaking wet, applauding one another for working it out.

There was an annoying sound coming from the sofa, so I checked it out only to discover it was Michael's cell phone. I grabbed it and jogged off to the guest room in the back so that I could hear.

"Hello?" I answered.

"Hi, this is Natasha. I need to speak with Michael."

Who did she think she was? She was speaking to me as if she was talking to the help. I looked up and Michael was standing in front of me. He knew the phone was for him.

"It's Natasha!" I said, handing him the phone. Michael smiled nervously and grabbed the phone. I stood back and observed and it was unbelievable—I watched him grow more excited as he spoke to her.

"Oh, yes that would be great, thanks for inviting me.

Sure, why not. Just call to remind me, and again, thanks." Michael hung up the phone. "That's the woman I was telling you about, my investor." Michael's face was searching for a better lie. "She was inviting me to a networking event. She wants to introduce me to some other cats with money to burn." Michael was beginning to stutter.

"And she couldn't wait to tell you. Had to call you right in the middle of our engagement party. Right?" I said, walking out of the room, not wanting to hear yet another lie.

I ran upstairs into the bathroom and began to cry. I couldn't hold it in any longer. There was a knock on the door.

"Baby, let me in." It was Granny. I looked in the mirror and I was a wreck. I wouldn't be able to hide this episode. I opened the door and let her in, then quickly shut and locked it. She grabbed me by the face.

"Spill it," she said.

"What if I don't marry Michael?" I questioned.

Suddenly, Granny brought up a deep-rooted memory of when I was seven years old and my mother was depressed after a man had left her, and she didn't send me and my little brother to school for five days. I was just a child, but I knew something wasn't right so I placed a secret phone call to my granny and told her what Mama was doing.

"I remember when I took y'all back to school and Sister Ann didn't think you would catch up on your schoolwork," Granny said as she took a seat on the edge of the tub. "I brought you and your brother back to my house. You had a week's worth of schoolwork piled up in front of you. Remember?" Granny said. It was all coming back to me. "From three o'clock in the afternoon until eight that night, you worked. Wouldn't even eat dinner until you were finished, and you did finish. Not one wrong answer either! Chile, you was determined to show Sister Ann and everybody else just how smart you were, yes sir!" Granny moved both of us with her words.

She pulled me to her and turned me toward the mirror. I saw little Charlie all over again with pigtails and a big grin, strong, determined, proud. As the image faded, I collected myself, dabbing my face with a hand towel.

"Chile, never let anything or *anyone* get in the way of your happiness or your dreams." She emphasized *anyone*. "Charlie, all we want is for you to be happy, and if Michael's not a part of your happiness, then so be it. Never mind everything else. You know what's for you, what's right or wrong. Just get back to that child that I know. When she puts her mind to something, she can do it!" Granny helped me to the door. "You ready?" she asked, giving me a kiss.

"Yes Granny, I'm ready," I said, marching out.

Chapter 28

Backsliding

Rule Number 4: Keep it moving, don't look back,
and don't let old memories trap you in the sack!

Charlie and I had been hanging tough, and since I hadn't seen Tara and Judy in a while, I invited them over. We'd bypass the fancy restaurant, so there was no need to dress up tonight. This was a chance to chill like we used to. However, I wouldn't dare tell them about all my escapades with Charlie. They would surely have me committed. As far as they knew I was still moping around, depressed over Troy, and busy with preproduction.

My kitchen was foreign territory, but I decided to try my hand at cooking. I had to christen these pans at some point in my lifetime. I racked my brain rifling through the pantry. I dusted off a box of pasta and a jar of spaghetti sauce. Boiling water couldn't be too hard.

Tara glanced over at the stove. "I think you should let the cooking thing go, Lin Lin."

"I wanted to make dinner for us," I said, unsure, looking at my pot of boiling salt water in disgust.

"I'll pass!" Judy sighed.

"I'm with Judy, Lin Lin."

"That's just rude, y'all!" I said, turning off the burner.

The phone rang.

"Lindsay?" a familiar voice asked.

"Troy?" My heart stopped. Judy's eyes widened and Tara started jumping up and down. I shushed them.

"I just wanted to hear your voice," he said.

"Oh, well, I'm kind of busy right now." A hint of nervousness ran through my voice. Judy and Tara were giving me silent animated signals not to screw things up.

"Look, I wanna see you."

"Oh, so you and your boy can play more games. I don't think so!"

"It's just dinner."

"Dinner. Hmmm? I don't know if that's a good idea, Troy." He did sound sincere, and I had to admit the anticipation of what it would be like to see him was palpable.

Tara and Judy were jumping up and down giving me "Are-you-out-of-your-mind-girl!" looks.

"Well, okay—sure!" I said enthusiastically. What would it hurt to see him over a little dinner on neutral territory? "Let's meet at Match," I suggested.

"Great. See you in about an hour."

By the time I hung up, Tara had pulled out my hottest three-inch-heel knee-high boots and Judy was holding up the tiniest skirt and T-shirt I owned.

"This is how you win, girlfriend, by looking hot!" Judy said, sucking her teeth. "You betta work it out and show Mr. Man everything he's been missing!"

Troy was standing outside the restaurant when I pulled up. I stepped out of the car in my Judy and Tara–inspired getup. Troy hugged me tightly.

"It's good to see you, L."

My body missed his touch. He was calling me L again. Okay, breathe! I had to remind myself of the Cosmo Code. *Keep it moving!* I can do this!

Match was a snug bar and grill in SoHo. Euro-eclectic music had us grooving at the bar. Troy whispered, "Let's do some shots." One shot quickly turned into four.

"Troy, what about Robin?"

"L., baby, let's just worry about me and you, please."

Bye-bye control! I was tangled in his words. We swayed to the rhythm of the music. Troy made me feel whole, womanly, desired. "I miss being with you so much," he said softly.

We stumbled down the steamy city streets. The night air slipped between our passionate kisses.

"Where are we going?" I asked.

"Trust me." Troy gave a lustful grin, and led me down the street.

The blue glow from a basement nightclub outlined our bodies. House music blared from inside. *Jack, Jack, Jack your body . . . Jack, Jack, Jack your body.* Troy pressed me against the wall and thrust his hips in between my legs. The little bit of skirt I was wearing was hiked up. My panties got wetter and wetter. I had to remember the Cosmo Code! *Don't let those good-ass memories trap me!* He pulled down my panties and began to penetrate me. I swear, I was trying hard not to go against the Code, but Troy, his touch, his eyes, were like Kryptonite.

I could hear drunken voices and snickers. I was so caught up I'd forgotten we were outside. Troy climaxed. I climaxed. We were certified exhibitionists.

"Let's go." Troy was moving too fast, and I was trying to catch my breath.

"Wait, where are we going now?" I asked.

Troy turned toward me. His green eyes were glowing. "We're going home," he whispered.

Troy sped over the Manhattan Bridge like lightning. Sade's lush vocals filled the car. Being with him again *was* the "Sweetest Taboo." My head was swimming with delight.

"I love you, Troy," I whispered.

Troy smiled. "Love you too," he said, pulling me closer and unlocking his front door. I had waited all this time to hear those words from him. It was worth the agony.

I walked into his house confidently. I scanned the room. The painting *Lay Your Heavy Burdens Down,* by Alonzo Adams, which I'd purchased for him, was hanging over the fireplace.

We tripped through the living room, now decorated and filled with beautiful furniture.

"Look familiar?" he said, pointing out the living room set. I picked it out one day while we were shopping, and now it was here. "You said it would look good." Troy gave me an endearing look.

We carefully made our way up the stairs to the master bedroom. I opened the door, shocked to see the room's new look. A beautiful cherrywood canopy bed fitted with Ralph Lauren's signature sheets was in the center of the room. I remembered when we used to make love on the small area rug because his old futon was too noisy and often messed with our rhythm. Why was I thinking about that? This was our reunion. I was about to reclaim my man! And I did, holding him tighter and tighter, as the fire bellowed between us.

The next morning Troy quietly rolled out of bed. I stirred and squinted against the sunlight streaming in through the blinds. He stood up and I eyed his naked backside hungrily. He reached for his shorts and sneakers, dressing for the gym. "Woman, have my breakfast ready when I get back," he joked. I threw a pillow at him and we both laughed. We were picking up right where we left off.

I hugged the sheets and sniffed them deeply. I wanted my skin to soak up his scent. I rolled over and out of the bed, tiptoeing gingerly across the cold wood floor to the bathroom. I wanted to shower and fix myself up before he got back.

I turned off the shower and wiped the fog from the sink mirror. I opened the medicine cabinet hoping to find one of my old barrettes or scrunchies. My jaw dropped at the sight of tampons, perfume, nail polish, and makeup—and none of it belonged to me. It all had to be Robin's, or some other woman's.

My brain was racing. Pandora's box had been opened and I knew there was more to be found. I flung open the closet in Troy's bedroom. Women's clothing hung near the back. This bastard has me up in here and he has a live-in girlfriend! And we hadn't used a condom. I hope to God I didn't catch anything. If I do I'll kill him!

A demon jumped in me and I started yanking out every piece of clothing I saw!

The laundry hamper was in the corner. I flipped it over, dumping all the contents out onto the floor. More women's clothing, even underwear. I ran back into the bathroom. Flinging open and slamming shut drawers and cabinets until I found the scissors. With one sweeping movement, I gathered all the clothes from the floor. I looked like Edward Scissorhands the way I masterfully cut everything into shreds and tiny bits. I was making sure the wrath of Lindsay would be felt. I caught my reflection in the large wall mirror. I looked like a madwoman but I didn't care. Thinking fast, I flew back into the bathroom, opened the drawer, and reached in to replace the scissors. I had to put everything back in order before Troy got back.

I discarded all the pieces of clothing into the bottom of the overturned hamper, then filled it back up with the soiled clothes. I grabbed a plastic bag from the kitchen and shoved an armful of the toiletries inside and stuffed them in the bottom of the garbage pail. By the time Troy returned, I was showered, dressed, and sitting on the couch waiting like an animal for its prey, waiting to pounce on him. I stared at the painting. It was supposed to be symbolic of my love.

Troy was glazed with beads of sweat, holding a bag of bagels and lox. He swooped in and gave me a gigantic bear hug.

"Whassup, L!" He smacked my buttocks. "I'm gonna shower. Breakfast is in the bag." He ran upstairs.

"Thanks, but I'm not hungry. I've got to get home to get some work done. I'll talk to you later." I headed for the door.

"Okay, cool, I'll hit you on the cell later."

I took one last look at the painting. A woman standing strong for her man as he bares his soul in her bosom. I had him right in front of me, face to face, and didn't open my mouth. Why was I afraid to confront him?

Chapter 29

Bamboozled

I was finally having my meeting with Miranda. I rehearsed my speech on the way to her office. Too bad Kyle was in L.A. on business. He'd have to get the news via e-mail. I knocked on Miranda's door.

"Charlie, please come in." Miranda opened the door and directed me to sit down.

Miranda, pretty, waiflike, and barely a day out of college, had worked her way up the corporate ladder horizontally, or so I heard.

"I just want to say thanks. The copy you wrote

was spectacular! The client absolutely loved it, as you already know."

I couldn't believe Miranda was finally giving me my due.

"Thank you for giving me the opportunity. I know you could have gone with Susan or another copywriter," I said, trying to play my corporate hand.

"They want more," Miranda said.

I was confused: was I getting a bonus or more work?

"Well, that's good to know. What can I do to help?"

"I'm so glad that you have this type of attitude, Charlie. Good copywriters are hard to come by. I could write the copy myself, but I'm swamped at the moment. So, I'm assigning you as the exclusive writer for the B-Cap account," Miranda said, walking over and patting me on the back.

I was thrown by her speech. Exclusive writer? I needed more details.

"That's great! When do I meet with the clients to discuss the specs?" I said cleverly, searching for more information. Miranda smiled as she handed me a piece of paper.

"Oh, you won't be meeting with them. Here are all the specs. If you have any questions, buzz me. Otherwise, I have complete faith in you. I know you will crank out the best possible copy." Miranda got up and returned to the other side of her desk.

"It's team spirit like this that will get you to the top, Charlie," Miranda said. I smiled uncomfortably and couldn't think of anything to say. I needed to leave Miranda's office right away. But as I headed out, she stopped me.

"Charlie, you're doing a great job." Miranda smiled as she picked up the phone.

"Thanks." If I was doing such a great job, where the hell was my bonus check? I want more money, not more work!

"Charlie, could you be a dear and shut my door behind you. Thanks, sweetie," Miranda said, returning to her phone call.

Slowly I walked back to my office. If looks could kill, everyone in sight would be dead. I noticed my phone line flashing and answered. It was Michael.

"Honey, I know this is short notice, but I have to make a trip to London." Michael was talking fast.

I was really confused. Miranda had just hit me with a left hook, and now Michael was coming with a right jab.

"I have to put in advance notice for vacation, I just can't pick up and leave," I said, wondering where all this was coming from.

"You don't need to go. It's a business trip," he said, and the phone was silent.

"Oh, I see." Michael was playing me for a fool, or at least he thought he was.

"Listen, the other night Natasha invited me to her annual networking party that she hosts at her home in London." Michael rattled off so much information I thought he was going to choke.

"Really," I said flatly.

"Look, I'm not going to argue with you about this. You'll just have to trust me. I just wanted to give you my flight information and find out how much money I need to withdraw for the monthly bills," Michael said coldly.

"You've already purchased your ticket?" I wanted to go off, but I was at work.

"If I was going to get the ticket at a decent price, I had

to get it today. Natasha's party is this Saturday." Michael was laid back and sure of himself. "Just tell me how much you need for the bills." Michael's voice began to crack.

"Michael, the bills are the same every month. Just leave me what you always leave."

"Cool, talk to you later. Love you."

He had his nerve saying those words to me. I didn't even dignify them with a response. This Natasha had my man wrapped around her pinky with this partnership scam. Her wealth had Michael's nose wide open.

Chapter 30

Detours

L indsay Bradley," I answered.

"Hey girl, it's me. I was wondering if we could move up the time for Girl's Night?"

"Let me see what I can do. What time were you thinking?" I asked.

"Now!"

"Something up?" I could hear trouble in Charlie's voice.

"One, I'm about to murder somebody at this job if I don't get out of here soon, and two . . ." Charlie paused and let out a deep sigh. "Lindsay, there's too much to tell over the phone."

"Calm down, I'll be there soon. I'm wrapping up now." I wanted to get to the Shark Bar in a hurry. This time Charlie needed me.

As I headed out of my office building, I spotted Shake's limo and tried to figure out a quick detour, but he caught me. He seemed drunk or high, just what I didn't need. I tried to be nice the other day when I called him to end our little affair. I hoped he wasn't here to make a scene. He yelled from the back window.

"A-yo, Lind-say, what's up? Why haven't you returned any of my calls?"

"Shake, what part of 'it's not gonna work' don't you understand. I'm sorry. I'm really busy and late for a meeting—"

By now he was out of the car. He cut me off, putting his finger in my face. I took a deep breath and backed up.

"Why you frontin' on me?" he badgered. "Do you know who I am? Shakediggity!" He stumbled slightly.

"Look, Shake, no one's frontin' on you, or whatever they call it," I tried to explain politely. "I simply discovered you aren't what I want or need in my life."

"Oh, but I was what you needed when you wanted to make your little punk-ass boyfriend jealous, right?"

"Get over it, Shake." I checked my watch.

"You probably back wit' his punk ass too."

"You *have* a woman. Not to mention, you're drunk. Go sleep it off or something."

"Fuck you, bitch!"

"Would you call your mother a bitch?"

I was mortified—we were right in front of my office. I could not be seen carrying on with this idiot. What if Robert walked out or someone else saw me?

"Could you please lower your voice, this is my office building."

"Fuck you and your job!" Shake was irate. Out of nowhere, Shake forcefully snatched me by the collar and pulled me toward him. His breath smelled like stale champagne. What he didn't realize was that he was pushing me back to my St. Louis roots, and I could get just as crazy. Forget my job, this was self-defense!

I pulled a Foxy Brown move and kneed him in the family jewels. "Urgh!" He winced and doubled over.

The sound of an oncoming police siren stopped us dead in our tracks. The wheels of an NYPD patrol car skidded to a halt. I was scared and so was Shake. He didn't need another blemish on his record. Before the cops could do anything, the radio went off and they were summoned to a real emergency. It was a close call. Shake ran and jumped into his car, and I started to speed walk in the other direction, but not before we wished each other well. "Fuck off!"

I made it to the Shark Bar and stormed through the door, still racing with adrenaline. Charlie was sitting at the bar. I told Stevie to give me a Cosmo and to keep them coming.

"I don't believe it, I just had to get violent on a brotha in front of my office."

"We know how the Lou gets, so that would've been real ugly," Charlie twisted a remark under her breath.

"Whatever! All I know is the Shake plan has officially backfired."

Stevie slid me a strong one. I painted an animated picture of the fight with Shake between sips.

"He actually tried to call me out about Troy. Like he would know about us hooking back up."

I tried to reach for my drink, but was caught. Charlie blocked it with her hand.

"I know you didn't get back with Troy."

"The dog!" Stevie exclaimed as his ears perked up.

"Excuse us!" we both shouted.

"Charlie, I didn't tell you because I know it was a weak move."

"But we made a deal to stick by each other no matter what."

"I was embarrassed."

"I'm your friend, you never have to be embarrassed with me."

I was stunned. No friend had ever said that to me. Just then my cell rang.

"What's up, Lindsay? It's Troy. How was your day?"

"My day was great, Troy." I perked up, signaling to Charlie. I noticed how he went from calling me L back to Lindsay.

"I'm glad I caught you," he said flatly.

"What's he saying to you?" Charlie mouthed.

"I'm glad you did too." I tried to play it off.

"Hey, since we're cool again, I wanted to invite you to my fight party tomorrow night."

"I'd love to come to *your* party, Troy," I said, making sure Charlie heard me.

"Cool, but I need to get something straight with you

first, about the other night at my house," Troy said, clearing his throat.

My armpits started to perspire and my hands felt clammy. Maybe he found the clothes? "What about it?" I asked defensively.

"I hope because of what happened you don't think we're going to just jump back into things again." Troy hadn't found the clothing, but he had obviously found his *cojones.*

"But you said you loved me, and told me how much you cared and missed me." I remembered, why didn't he?

"I don't know about all that, but a brotha might say anything when he's drunk and horny," Troy chuckled. I was quiet, angered by his flippant behavior and my own imbecility.

"C'mon Lindsay, you were barely standing up yourself, and you know you get freaky when you're drunk."

I couldn't believe he was turning our night together into a one-night stand.

"I just want us to be adult about this. I don't want you assuming we're gonna be a couple. Feel free to bring someone, too. I'll have a date myself. I hope I'm being clear."

I thought he was done but he wasn't.

"And another thing, I don't want you to be out at three A.M. drunk, thinking it's okay for you to call me or to come over my house," Troy said.

I wanted to go through the phone and slap the life out of him. "I mean quiet as it's kept. I haven't forgotten about what you did to me. I have to say that I'm not entirely sure that I can trust you. I need more time. Until then, do us both a favor and *please* don't start trippin' again." Troy was getting a bit too cocky and it was the final straw.

"Believe me, I won't. That's the *last* thing you'll have to worry about." I pressed end and turned to Charlie.

"Go ahead and say it."

"Say what?"

"I told you so."

"Nah, I won't say that, but I will say that we have to both promise never to go against the Cosmo Code of Arms again. Okay?"

"Fine! Troy has some nerve, though. Can you believe he invited me to his party and told me I could bring a date, because he was bringing one? I bet it's that girlfriend whose stuff I saw at his house." I was furious.

"What girlfriend? What stuff?"

"I found a bunch of women's clothing in Troy's closet, but I'm glad I cut all of it up!"

"Whoa, back up. No, you didn't?"

"Yes, I did! Charlie, what burns me up is that I really loved Troy." I was getting emotional.

"Don't you dare start crying. He's not worth it. You should shock the hell out of him and show up with Stevie."

"No way! I'm not going at all. Seeing him with her would really drive me over the edge. I'll feel like crap, and he'll be partyin' it up. It's not fair!"

"I didn't want to get ugly, but this snake is asking for it." Charlie yanked out her cell phone. "Stevie, let me borrow your pen. Lindsay, hand me a napkin." Charlie ordered, quickly grabbing both from us, dialing information. "Two numbers, in Brooklyn, Con Edison and Verizon. Thanks!" Charlie jotted down the numbers, and began dialing. "Lindsay, write down Troy's info, hurry!" Charlie said, clearing her throat. "Yes, is this Con Ed? Great! I'm moving out of the country, and I need to disconnect my service immediately!" she said, folding her arms, glaring at me.

Charlie was on the warpath, and anything that had to do with Troy was getting rolled over. I guess my wicked ways have rubbed off on her. "That's why you're my girl! Show that dog St. Louis and Buffalo don't play!" I said proudly, raising my glass.

"So much for Troy's little party," Charlie said.

Suddenly, it dawned on me that Charlie needed to talk, but my drama had distracted us.

"Wait, Charlie, I'm sorry. What's going on with you? Something about work and you couldn't say the rest."

"It's nothing. Just a tiny thing at the office," Charlie said nonchalantly.

"You sure? You seemed troubled about more than just a 'tiny thing' at work." I didn't want to press, but I felt Charlie was holding something back.

"I've turned into the ghostwriter for my boss and I'm not going to get any more money or any recognition for doing her work. Plus, this white chick who doesn't even have as much experience as I do just got a bonus," Charlie said in a huff.

"You know from jump that as a black person and a woman we're cursed with a double whammy! In corporate America it's the white male who has all the power. Women, black and white, need to start realizing that. That's the enemy and we need to work together to bring him down, not each other."

"But, Lindsay, I'm tired of paying dues."

"Me too, but get used to it. We're gonna be paying dues for the rest of our lives. You just got to let it roll off your back like water off a duck, and be positive."

"Or get to calling Johnny Cochran!"

"Forget suing. If they don't give you what you want, someone else will. Get your writing samples and portfolio together. Promote yourself. You know your craft, claim it and go in there to win! You can start by walking into your boss's office and asking for that bonus."

"Come out with it, just like that?" Charlie asked.

"Absolutely, but be smart. Let her know you're concerned, and that it reflects poorly on company politics if you're doing all this wonderful work and not being recognized or compensated. Trust me, she'll get the hint!"

"Well, all right!"

"Charlie, I have an idea. Let's get started on putting your portfolio together. I've got a lot of experience with this kind of stuff. How's my place next girls' night?"

"That's the best proposal I've had all year," Charlie said with a half-smile.

"Well, don't get too excited," I replied, with a slightly acerbic tone.

"No, girl, I really am excited but I just thought about Michael again. He upset me at work."

"He's always upsetting you. Don't tell me he's working overtime again."

"Yeah, something like that. I guess I just wish he were

home more often. It'll be all right. I'm also stressed from work, and getting ready for the wedding. I'll be fine."

"You sure, Charlie?"

"Positive."

I could tell she was done talking for now, so I didn't push her.

Chapter 31

I Am My Sister's Keeper

L ook how good you look on paper!" I said,
handing Charlie her revamped portfolio.

"Wow, I didn't realize how valuable I was until now. Thanks, girl!"

I headed into the kitchen to get us both seconds of the heartburn feast, steak pizziola and
onion rings, that Charlie had cooked. I decided
to whip up a batch of my best Cosmos. Charlie
checked out the rest of my apartment.

"I really like your place, Lindsay," she said,
walking into the kitchen holding a small silver
frame. "Still hanging on, huh?"

"Oh yeah. I thought I threw that out with the others," I said sheepishly. But I knew I hadn't, I was holding on to it for sentimental value.

"Lindsay, I know we had fun getting back at Troy, but how are you, truthfully? I know you really loved him," Charlie said, sitting down at the small bistro table.

"Past tense is right!" I grabbed a chair, poured two glasses, and began to sip slowly. I hadn't given Charlie all the particulars until now. "We didn't use a condom that night," I said solemnly.

"What! Lindsay, what were you thinking with AIDS and HIV out here? You know you've got to be extra careful." Charlie was fearful.

"I know. I wasn't thinking. I made an appointment with my gynecologist already." I paused. "Charlie girl, I've really gotten out of hand. This isn't me. If my family knew what Miss Big City was really doing, they'd be disgusted." I tried to laugh it off but it really wasn't funny. Charlie cracked a smile. "But you know what! I'm done being hung up on Troy. In fact, I've got a surprise for you!" I said, rushing off to the bedroom. Within seconds I returned. "I'm back on the job!" I placed an armload of bridal magazines in front of Charlie. "That killer dress is in here somewhere."

Charlie didn't say a word, she just stared. She began to weep and I grabbed a handful of Kleenex.

"Why are you crying? My life is the one that's in shambles, not yours, dummy." I tried to stop her from crying.

"In the beginning it's all about you. You fall in love, put up with their tomfoolery and their shortcomings, and then, just like that, the next thing you know they're off to London ready to replace you with some old, rich broad." Charlie patted her tears dry then took a big gulp from her Cosmo.

"Are you telling me that Michael is sleeping around on you?"

"I haven't been completely honest, Lindsay. My frustration with Michael isn't just about working so much and never being home. I've been in denial for a long time. Michael is cheating on me. Her name is Natasha, she's French and white!"

"Oh my God! Charlie, are you sure?"

"I'm sure *now*. All I had at first was a bunch of prank calls. Then, the day I met you in the Shark Bar I went to his job and he wasn't there. He blatantly lied about his whereabouts. And this trip to London is all the proof I need. He's there with her!"

"I can't believe you've been dealing with this all by yourself. I know I can be in my own world at times but did you feel like you couldn't confide in me?"

"Lindsay, I was serious when I told you I'm not used to the whole female-bonding thing. I don't think I've had a *real* girlfriend since high school. I may share little things with Kyle and my granny, but I deal with the big problems on my own."

"Not anymore, we're going to deal with this together. I got your back, you understand?"

"Yes ma'am!"

"Good! Now I am going to ask you once more, are you sure?" I questioned.

Charlie was resigned and folded her arms across her chest. "As sure as my heart beats."

I always thought the grass was greener on the other side, but now I was finding out that it was the same lawn.

The masquerade was over. Charlie let go like a patient on a therapist's couch. "This is the reward I get after baby-sitting all his issues, giving him my all," Charlie said, closing her eyes and continuing. "I've been going through so much with this man. Mostly because he's not a man, he's really a boy. He had those two kids with Juanita, never married her, and lived with his mama until he moved in with me. I knew that it was a mistake, but just like you, my heart ached," Charlie admitted.

Sista girl was in a hell of a quandary. It was obvious Charlie had let her displeasure and frustration with Michael fester. Purging herself of all this pain was long overdue.

"It's always the same story with him. Something new or just plain adult, normal things, turn Michael out. When he got his new truck, he thought he was a baller! So he had to hang out with the boys every night for two months straight." Charlie started to laugh at herself. "While I was at home being his superwoman, running a household and taking care of *his* kids. Now the ungrateful bastard is cheating on me!"

"Brothas kill me! I bet she wouldn't be so quick to take him if she knew about all his baggage!" I was heating up.

"I have another confession. It's been over two months since we've had sex." Charlie looked up at me.

"Charlie, shut up!" I was outdone.

"It's true. I've been lying in that bed just dry-rotting and I'm supposed to believe that he and Natasha only have a business relationship. She's helping him start his own construction business, and ten days alone with her in her mansion in London is only about networking!" Charlie rolled her eyes. "You know, Lindsay, I grew up in a house with a mother who was truly a man's fool. That woman acted like she couldn't do anything unless she had a man in her life," Charlie said with disdain.

"But nothing's wrong with not wanting to be alone," I interjected, refilling her glass.

"No, girl. She would get downright depressed when she didn't have a man, and when she did get one, look out! She would roll out the red carpet and treat him like he was a king—even if he didn't deserve it. Just as long as she had a man, that's all that mattered. I said I'd never end up like her, now look at me," Charlie said, holding her drink.

"Awh, girl, I can't hear no more. What are you gonna do?" I said, pacing the floor.

"I just want to pack up and leave," Charlie said.

"Why do you have to leave? It's your apartment. Kick his sorry butt out!"

"Too many years with him in that place. When I leave him, I want to leave everything connected to him. Only thing, a fresh start is expensive. I only got a few dollars saved, how am I gonna afford to move?"

"What am I, chopped liver? You've had my back more than all my so-called other girlfriends put together. Not to mention helping me with this Troy crap. And we're going to find you a place you can call home. Don't worry about money, I got you," I stated with authority.

"You don't have to do that. Just helping me find a place while I save money is enough."

"Will you shut up already and let me do this. Just drink, before it gets warm."

The tables had turned. Charlie always seemed to be the pillar of strength whenever we were together but now I was fired up.

"It's time to make some amendments to our Code of Arms, Miss Charlie. Rule five is to do something daring and deliciously drastic; rule six is you've got to let go and live." I was pacing furiously. "Now, who makes it all possible?"

"Nobody else but the Almighty himself!" Charlie shouted.

"That's right, and God gave you two feet, so you'd better stand on them. That's rule number seven. And last but certainly not least, number eight: you'd better throw that mental mess with Michael out with the rest of the garbage and start fresh! Now, hello, will the real Charlie Thornton please stand up!"

"Girlfriend, here I am and I'm back!" Charlie stood up and did her own victory dance right in my kitchen.

"So, in keeping true to our new Code, tomorrow is Three-D day! Our first new mission," I stated.

"And just where are we going to do all this daring and deliciously drastic stuff?"

"Miss Charlie, you'd better recognize. I've got this! We're going to Bliss and we're going to get pampered for an entire day!" I said, refilling our glasses.

Just then the phone rang.

"I don't think you're ready to be a producer on a big series," Robert's voice blared.

I stopped dead in my tracks. "I'm sorry, come again?" I

was reaching for pen and paper to take notes and knocked over my glass, spilling all the contents into my plate, but I still kept a calm, professional tone. My face dropped: Robert was telling me that he had decided to bring in a producer from some network show to produce *my* show.

"Why, Robert? This is my project!"

"And I've got networks to run. We could kill in the ratings if we do this right. You don't have the experience, Lindsay." Robert's decision was final. I didn't have any way to challenge him.

"I understand." I was defeated.

"Lindsay, I need you to be a team player on this. See you Monday morning ten A.M. sharp."

"No problem." I hung up and collapsed into my chair. My anger couldn't be contained. I broke free and began pacing again.

"He's such an asshole!"

"What happened?"

"Robert took my series away from me. He said I wasn't ready. This was my big chance, Charlie."

"Why didn't you hold your ground?" Charlie asked.

"I don't know. Maybe I was scared."

"You know, Lindsay, you give one hundred percent to your job and one hundred percent to a man, but you never give Lindsay anything. Did you read that book I gave you?" Charlie looked around the room searching for it.

"Please, I am not listening to the preachings of some one-dollar lesson on self-assertive behavior." I had actually perused the book's tattered pages numerous times, but I wasn't going to tell her that. "Can we forget about the book?" I begged.

"Yes, for now. But what if I say you need rule five more than me?"

"Bliss isn't going to solve my problems," I said flatly.

"Maybe not, but it's a start," Charlie retorted.

A smile managed to find its way into my eyes.

Chapter 32

Three-D Day

*Rule Number 5: Do something daring
and deliciously drastic.*

The number on the building read 568, but the building didn't appear to be a typical spa. Charlie and I entered and caught the elevator just as it was closing. As the car climbed, the smell of sea salt and eucalyptus filtered in. We gave each other encouraging smiles, definitely a sign a spa was near.

Billie Holiday was crooning "Fine and Mellow." Bright fluorescent white lights showed off the spa products on the wall shelves. The employees, dressed in black pants and white shirts and aprons, were jolted with energy and looked more like waiters than spa attendants.

"Ladies, welcome. Lindsay, sweetie, you're on this floor and Sienna will be your massage therapist. And Charlie, you're upstairs," our check-in attendant said cheerfully.

I followed the blue-and-white wall guides to my locker. The locker room was relatively empty. I put down my purse and let out a deep sigh. *Today was officially Three-D day*. A new adventure was certainly *daring*, and you couldn't get any more *delicious* than self-pampering.

I was naked and about to slip into a thin waffled cotton robe when my cell rang. I'd forgotten to turn it off. "Yeah," I said in an unfriendly tone.

"Lindsay, I wanted to get you early. I'm out of pocket later," Robert said.

The massage therapist came around the corner and called my name, "Lindsay?" I hesitated and asked Robert to hold on as I covered the phone. "Yes, I'm right here," I called back to her.

"Good morning, I'm Sienna. Are you ready?"

"Not exactly . . ."

"I'm sorry, no cell phones." Sienna could see I was trapped between my phone call and my purpose for being here.

"I'm turning it off now," I said, apologetically.

"I'll come back and then we'll start over," Sienna whispered. I reluctantly finished my call.

"Robert, unfortunately this is not a good time for me. Could you just give me a couple of hours?"

The fact this was *my* Saturday meant nothing to him.

"Lindsay, I'm extremely busy. I'm the CEO of a billion-dollar business, in case you haven't noticed. I've got budgetary concerns about this pilot, we're getting closer to the shoot, and I can't work around your schedule."

I didn't utter a response. I swallowed my repugnance, remembering a quote from the book, breathing in for one—*Okay, Stand Up, Speak Out, Talk Back! I am going to express my anger constructively*—now breathe out for two. "Robert, I wasn't expecting your call, and I'm in the middle of an appointment. I can't talk."

"Look, I may have a few minutes around four, you can try me then on my cell," Robert said and hung up.

What do you know, the book actually worked. That damn Charlie! I pressed power and tossed my cell into my locker.

I lay still, facedown, drifting in and out of dreamland on the massage table. The warmth from the heated pad cuddled my nude body. The blue-green textures on the walls and floor were soothing and made me feel like I was near the ocean. Sienna lightly brushed my skin with her fingertips from head to toe.

Sienna worked my shoulder blades, arms, thighs, and every muscle slowly and deeply. Eucalyptus and lemongrass vapors lulled me into a deep sleep.

Next, I found myself sitting in the steam room. Still. Alone. I inhaled and exhaled deeply again, slinking into the thick, mentholated clouds. I could hear my mama's voice: *When you don't know what to say or do, just stand. Stand steadfast and be still. God will speak to you.*

My life was at a low: I don't remember the last time I called my family, and I've almost lost my self-respect because of a man and a decadent lifestyle of sex and alcohol. Enough was enough.

Where was the girl who came to take on New York, who was grounded and humble? I knew better and I'd have a hell of a price to pay if I didn't get my act back together and get back to what had gotten me this far: God and my family.

Charlie and I met at the checkout desk.

"I feel great. What about you, how do you feel?" Charlie asked.

"Uplifted and divine!" I said.

Later that night, we sat at a cozy table on the mezzanine of Town overlooking the twinkling bar and tables below. Town was tucked away discreetly inside the sumptuously modern Chambers Hotel. Sexy and very cosmopolitan, to match the fresh round we were elegantly sipping on. The quiet electricity of the city penetrated the walls. Festive people milled about the opulent bilevel restaurant.

The remnants of an elaborate spread of sea bass, salmon, escargot, leeks, and imported cheeses sat before us. We were basking in the afterglow of being queens for a day.

"I decided I'm ready to take the blinders off and start seeing my life and actions with clarity, with twenty-twenty vision. How about you?" I said.

"I know now that nobody's going to block my path in life. I'm the captain of my own ship."

"You took the words right out of my mouth, girlfriend!" I interjected.

The waitress approached with the check and we gagged at the total. There was one part of Three-D day I'd forgotten to fulfill. I whipped out my brand-new platinum Visa like lightning. "This is for something drastic!" I said, putting all three hundred bucks of our meal on my card. "To having good credit!" I winked.

We laughed and got comfortable for a few more glasses.

Chapter 33

Corporate Takeover

Today was the first day of shooting on the Alix Alexander pilot, *City Heat*. Robert hadn't given me my stripes to produce, but I had to remain professional. However, my future at the company depended heavily on this meeting.

Robert was a half hour late for the meeting I set up, but as much as I wanted to cancel there was no turning back. I stayed up half the night cramming verses from the text of *Stand Up, Speak Out, Talk Back!* into my brain. It reminded me of my red-eyed college study sessions before a big exam.

I couldn't afford for the pocket-sized, worn pages to fail me now. I had to be confident. I reviewed a verse from the book: *"I can prevent or remedy the little murders which are an ever-present threat to my self-respect."*

I was busy staring out at the view, rehearsing my lines when Robert entered and loudly put down his coat and briefcase, startling me.

"What's up, Lindsay? You needed to talk?"

"Uh yes, I, umm . . ."

I swallowed hard, remembering the cheat sheet I'd prepared—just in case I got stuck.

"Robert, I've recently reassessed some key professional issues and have come to a conclusion." Robert stared at me blankly. I paused. "A change is needed as it relates to my role here at the company, but more importantly, in my relationship with you."

I caught myself. I was being too formal and academic. Robert was too busy for a bunch of words. The main message of the book began to pour from my memory: *a person will "respect and work hard for the assertive supervisor who is as free with praise as with criticism, who treats an employee as a valuable human being without patronizing."* My delivery suddenly became poised and relaxed. I was putting my cards on the table today, by any means necessary, and he wasn't leaving until I was finished.

"I'm your most loyal employee in this company, but we're going to have to set some parameters."

"So shoot . . ."

Robert nonchalantly whipped out his Palm Pilot, jotted down a note of some sort, walked over to his desk, and sat down. I was thrown. All this moving around was distracting. He was giving off negative vibes and ignoring me, but I knew his game. My anger was brewing.

"I already strive for perfection and put enough pressure on myself. I don't need you making matters worse." Robert looked up. I'd finally gotten his attention. "I like that you push me, and you give great advice most of the time, but you're going to have to respect that I exist outside these walls."

"Is that it?"

"Well, no. I want to produce the Alix Alexander series. It was my idea. I got the talent. I have the vision."

"It was a major undertaking and you weren't—"

"I know you think I'm not ready." Now I was doing the cutting off for a change. "Robert, how am I ever going to be ready if I'm not given a chance?"

"I'm not running a lab, Lindsay."

"I don't want a handout."

"What do you want?"

"I want some respect. I want to prove myself."

Robert stood up abruptly and pounded his fist on his desk. "I didn't become this successful letting my staff call the shots. You just gave a nice speech, but it's time to step back into the real world, Lindsay. We've got work to do."

Things had gotten more heated than I had anticipated. I took another deep breath.

"Look, put me in charge of my own show. Please, Robert." I was begging Robert for something that was rightfully mine. Robert's intercom buzzed. He made it a point to put his assistant on speaker.

"Mark Peters is here. He says it's urgent. Alix won't report to set."

"Lindsay, I need to talk to *our* producer." I was free to go.

I didn't know what to make of the meeting, or what I had accomplished. I wondered if I'd just made a fool of myself. Part of me felt exhilarated: I'd finally spoken up for myself. But the other side of me was totally dejected. Had I been insubordinate? I feared Robert would give me a demotion just to get back at my big mouth. I swallowed my pride and graciously exited Robert's office.

Turns out I was pulled into Mark's little emergency anyway. Tensions were high on set. Alix was two hours late for her first shot of the day. She was refusing to leave the hair and makeup trailer.

"I hate this fucking scene, Lindsay!" Alix said, yelling from the makeup chair, throwing the script across the room.

"Alix, calm down. Just talk to me. Everything is fixable," I said in a clear, direct tone. Mark Peters anxiously shifted as he stood next to me. Just then Robert entered the trailer.

"Good afternoon, Alix. I hear we're having some problems," he said. Robert was terrible at hiding the fact he had no patience for temperamental actresses.

"Alix, I'm sure if we can just get this first shot off . . ." Mark butted in, as if Alix were interested in negotiating with him.

"What part of "I-hate-this-fucking-scene" don't you understand? You are useless! Just shut up. I'm talking to Lindsay."

Alix had turned into a nightmarish, Hollywood Diva right before my eyes.

"Alix, yelling isn't going to get us anywhere. I realize you've had three previous conversations about the scene, but I wasn't a part of those." I casually cut my eye at Robert. "But I can assure you, we'll fix the scene together, and it will be what you want," I said, turning to the production assistant standing with a headset on. "Please, bring Ms. Alexander some peppermint tea," I asked, before returning my attention to Alix. "It'll help relax you, girl." I was speaking a language she understood.

"Fine! I have my suggestions in my dressing room. Thank you, *Lindsay*," Alix said, rolling her eyes at Mark and Robert. I knew that Robert didn't care one bit about Alix's little tantrum. In his head, he was counting up the hundreds of thousands of dollars Alix was costing production for the delay.

An hour later, the scene met Alix's approval and we were back on schedule. I was standing in front of a camera monitor, and Robert walked up beside me.

"Good job handling Alix earlier."

"Underneath all the glam and drama, Robert, actors and actresses just want to feel like their opinions matter. The key is to give them an ear and let them know someone is listening," I said, without taking my eyes off the monitor.

"Excuse me, Lindsay. Can you take a look at the wardrobe for the next scene?" the costume designer politely interrupted.

"Sure thing, on my way."

As I turned to follow her, Robert touched my arm. "Keep up the good work, Lindsay."

"Always!" I said confidently before walking away.

Chapter 34

Let the Games Begin

I'm sure Michael enjoyed his ten-day stay in London. Being waited on hand and foot by servants and staying in a five-bedroom mansion. He made sure to call and tell me all about it. Michael was living out most men's fantasies.

I heard Michael pull into the driveway. *I bet he still smells of her. I bet he's smiling to himself thinking he's real clever, how he got over on me.* I heard him creeping down the stairwell, slowly inserting the key into the lock. He would think I was asleep. After all, I was predictable and never broke my routine. He entered the apartment and placed his suitcase down by my desk. Just like me, his routine was the same. As usual, Michael headed directly to the kitchen to eat the soulful meal I usually slaved over. What he wasn't expecting was for the kitchen to be clean and closed for the night. I heard him open the fridge searching. No leftovers for you, my dear! He was shocked when he passed the bedroom, and instead of hearing my snoring he heard an upbeat breathing pattern.

I was in the midst of an intense workout, sweating away to Billy Blank's *Taebo Live*. I was wearing a brand-new spandex suit that revealed the certain truth that I really didn't need to exercise. I simply wanted to.

I peeked at Michael; he was at a loss for words and attempted to get my attention. I'd heard him when he parked in the driveway, but he'd interrupted my life for the last time. Michael had no choice but to speak first.

"Hey, baby. Looking good," he said, trying hard to figure out what was going on.

"Hey, glad to see you made it back safely." I was dismissive. I walked right past Michael and turned off the tape.

"I guess you ate already, huh?" He was apprehensive as he searched for his next words.

"Yes, I did, thanks for asking." I left Michael standing puzzled in the hallway, his mouth open. Huh! He was going to have to get a full stomach of disappointment tonight. I went into the bathroom, shutting and locking the door behind me.

I took a long lavish shower, paying extra attention to every part of my body. I went into the laundry room, opened up my lingerie drawer and decided: *not tonight, dear.* I grabbed my favorite oversized Tweety Bird cotton T-shirt.

Michael was undressed and waiting in bed. I entered the bedroom and Michael's look was priceless. He was expecting Victoria's Secret, but tonight I had a secret of my own. *I'm leaving your tired useless ass.* I couldn't help but smile at the thought.

Michael misread me and smiled back. I never saw him like this before. Michael was truly one pathetic man. I was so turned off I felt drier than the Sahara Desert. I hit the light switch before climbing into bed, and this time, for the first time, I rolled over, giving Michael my back.

"Sleep tight."

Chapter 35

God Bless the Child

I took off from work for my gynecologist appointment. My doctor didn't have another opening until next month, so there was no way I was missing it. I washed my hands in the sink, praying I didn't have an STD. My doctor and I had a relaxed relationship and called each other by our first names.

"What's the verdict, Nancy?" My face was fear-stricken.

"Which one?" she asked. Nancy cleared her throat. "Lindsay, your Pap smear checked out. You're clean." She paused. "But you are pregnant."

"Pregnant?" My eyes puddled up.

"You're about four weeks." Nancy took another pause. "Lindsay, I know you stopped taking the pill last year to give your body a break from all the toxins, but I had no idea you were trying to get pregnant."

"I wasn't. The last thing I want is to have a baby right now."

"But we've talked about condoms and other methods of birth control. What happened?"

"Nancy, please, no speeches. You're my doctor and I trust you, but I've got a lot to think through. It was my fault. I listened to a foolish heart and not a lucid mind."

"If it helps, you're not alone. So not just as your doctor, but as your friend, when you're ready let me know and we'll talk about your next step," she said, patting my hand. "Take your time leaving."

I had to get out of that office fast, get some air, try to figure all this out. I stopped and sat on a park bench and watched a group of small children playing. I opened my cell and dialed.

"Hi, it's Lindsay."

"Oh, good, Angie's over too." Faith pulled the phone away and called out, "Angie, pick up the phone. It's our long lost sister, Lindsay."

"Hey, girl." Angie sounded concerned. "Where have you been? What did the doctor say?"

"I know, I'm sorry, but it's bad y'all." I burst into tears. "I'm pregnant."

"You have to tell Troy," Faith said, keeping a level head.

"We're not together," I said, blubbering.

"Lindsay, what were you thinking?" Angie questioned.

"I don't need this from you, Angie! You act like you've never made a mistake. You don't want me to throw all your bad decisions in your face, namely your own damn child!"

I'd crossed the line. Angie's son's father disappeared when she got pregnant and wouldn't even claim my nephew until he was five years old. She had a fit at first but then took him back like a fool after he'd gone out and started another family, but they were happily married now. What I'd just done was taboo. No one in our family ever brought up her situation. Angie slammed the phone down. That was the end of that. I knew we wouldn't be speaking for a while, again.

"Lindsay, now you know you were wrong. You're hurting but that's no reason to strike out at your family. We love you, and you know how emotional Angie gets." Faith tried to calm me down.

"I'm sorry, but my life is screwed right now!" I was crying and screaming at the top of my lungs. "I have a career! What am I going to do with a baby?"

"We are your family, Lindsay, and we will help you take care of the baby."

"Are you kidding me? You don't understand. You've never been in my shoes, Faith. I have a plan for my life!" I was striking out at everyone.

"Well, you should've thought about that before!" Faith yelled.

"I'm getting rid of it!"

"What! You can't have an abortion. A woman in your position has no excuse." Faith paused and lowered her voice. "You need to relax and pray. Ask God for strength.

Lindsay, you know how to pray if you don't know how to do anything else."

"I gotta go!" I said and hung up. I just couldn't be a single mother.

I was always so determined to get what I wanted in my life, but now I had to take a hard look at my life. I needed God more than ever, but I wouldn't allow myself to see that. I got up and started my long walk home.

I was in my first trimester and having a hard time, light-headed from throwing up all afternoon. Lying in bed recuperating, I figured now was as good a time as ever to tell Troy about the baby. Even if I wasn't going to keep it, he had a right to know. I slowly dialed his number.

"Hello?" A woman's voice answered on the other end. "Hello?" she asked again and I paused. It sounded like she was still in bed. "Um, hello, is Troy in?" I finally answered.

"Hold on a sec."

I was trying to hold myself together to handle business. Troy fumbled with the receiver.

"Hello?"

"Troy, um, it's Lindsay. We need to talk."

"Can this wait? I'm kinda busy right now."

I wasn't going to let what was happening on the other end stop me from getting out what I needed to say.

"Look, I need to see you."

"Why don't you just call me later?"

I didn't want it to be this way, but he was forcing me.

"I'm pregnant, Troy."

He was quiet at first, then he chuckled. "Fine, how much do these things cost now? Three, four hundred?"

I was astounded. Clearly, my situation wasn't new to him. Troy offered up money, like he knew he could write me off at whatever the cost.

"You can't be serious?"

"I'm very serious, Lindsay. By the way, I saw the clothes you cut up."

"Troy, did you just hear what I said?"

"And did you just hear what I said? Look, it's all good. I know you were under a great deal of mental anguish after we broke up. I'm gonna let it all slide," Troy said with sarcasm. "This conversation's over, Lindsay."

He hung up and I threw the phone across the room with a vengeance. I crawled out of bed nauseous and dizzy. I was thunderstruck by what had just happened. Did I ever know Troy at all? I made it to the bathroom just in time as vomit spewed from my mouth. After what seemed to be an eternity, I collapsed on the bathroom floor and cried until I fell asleep.

My body jolted from the sound of the train passing. My chest was heaving. I dragged myself to the patio door, opened it, and stepped out onto the balcony for some air. The world circled around me. Troy was ruthless, cold, and what was happening with me didn't matter. He didn't want a relationship with me or the baby. Out of frustration, I screamed as loud as I could, but the city's noise was too overpowering and drowned me out.

Chapter 36

Movin' On Up

Lindsay turned onto Ninety-eighth and River-side Drive. This was our seventh apartment go-see for the week. We could have seen more, but our shopping and eating breaks were so much more enjoyable. "This ad sounds like a winner. Lord knows I'm ready to escape from Michael's prison. Lindsay, it's getting harder to ig-nore a person who really doesn't give a damn about you anyway!" I said, neatly folding up the newspaper.

"Charlie, you're being dramatic again—"

"Michael believes he's so much more. Why

can't he get it through his thick head? She doesn't give a damn about him," I angrily interrupted.

"When girlfriend finds out you left him, and she can have him all to herself, that's when the game will be over and he'll realize what he had, but it'll be too late. There's no better time than the present to remember rule number seven: 'God gave you those two feet, so stand on them, girl'!'" Lindsay said, reassuring me.

She pulled up in front of a prewar building. I could see the old-fashioned elevator from the street. I had always dreamed of living in a building with an elevator like this. I double-checked the address in the ad. It was correct. Lindsay was thinking the same thing, as she put on her glasses, triple-checking the information.

"So far so good." Lindsay gave an affirming nod and turned the car off.

"Too good to be true is more like it. I love this block. Reminds me of *The Cosby Show* with all these brownstones." I surveyed the street. I was wound up to get inside. "If the outside is any indication of what the actual apartment looks like, this place is mine," I said, feeling optimistic.

We walked up the front stairs and I pressed the doorbell as we crossed our fingers for luck. A tall white-haired man in his late sixties appeared.

"Hello, I'm Mr. Baxter and you must be Charlie? You're on time too, I like that," he said, shaking our hands, welcoming us inside. The place was beautiful. The wooden accents looked historic and classy.

"I don't live here anymore. Retired and can't take the bitter winters. I'm living in Florida now. That's why I'm letting it go for such a cheap price," he said.

The master bedroom was stark white, bright, and warm from the sun. *My own piece of heaven*, I thought. The bathroom had an antique tub and a modern shower, but they somehow matched perfectly. There was another room that was big enough for an office or a small second bedroom. The kitchen was brand new. All the appliances were black and chrome, my favorite.

"Mr. Baxter, I want this apartment," I said confidently.

"Do you smoke, have a pet, or kids or a boyfriend?" he quizzed.

"No, no, double no, and not anymore I'm pleased to say." I played right into his game.

"Then you should be as quiet as a church mouse and clean as a nun," Mr. Baxter laughed. Lindsay and I followed his lead. I would have done cartwheels if he wanted me to, anything for this apartment.

"I do love playing my music, and every now and then I let my laundry pile up," I said.

"You're honest. That's good. If your application pans out, I see no reason why you can't have it," he said.

I shook his hand graciously. "Don't worry, it will pan out. Do you mind if we take another look around?"

"No problem. I'll be waiting outside in my car."

He left, and as soon as the coast was clear we let out big screams.

"I love it! I must be dreaming. This place is perfect." I dipped back into the spare room. Lindsay followed.

"I could finally have a real office."

"Or this could serve as a second bedroom for your godson or goddaughter when they spend the weekend," Lindsay said under her breath, then let loose a big smile.

"A what? What did you say? I don't have a godson or goddaughter."

"Not yet, but you will in about six months from now."

Lindsay was happy, but I couldn't help it, I had to be some kind of sounding board for her. "No, no, no. Don't tell me Shake is the father?"

"No way! I doubled up on the condoms with him," Lindsay laughed, then it hit me.

"Oh my God, it's Troy's."

"Yes, and I know what you're thinking. Don't worry. I went to see my gynecologist. I'm STD-free," Lindsay said defensively.

"I'm happy you don't have a disease, but sista, you're in the dark. You think having his kid is going to make you and Troy live happily ever after?" I was concerned. Lindsay was not seeing the light.

"Wait a minute! I'm not using this pregnancy to get back with him. I don't even want Troy back, but I do want this baby."

"I'm not trying to rain on your parade, but you've been through a lot of shit with that jerk. Are you sure you want to have his baby? And do you really think Troy will be co-operative at this point?" I asked, hoping she would see how messed up things would be.

"Like I said, it's not about him. But I know he will understand and, in the end, he'll do right by us," Lindsay said without wavering.

"Really? Your entire relationship with Troy was based on lies. The brotha just dogged you in the worst way."

"Can we move on already!"

"What is it, Lindsay, that's making you do this? Love,

ego, insecurity?" I couldn't understand her irrational behavior.

"Look, I'm not getting any younger. I'm planning to buy
a place and now I'll have the baby. I may never get the husband, but two out of three isn't bad. Charlie, it's my baby
and I want to keep it. Trust me, I know what I'm doing.
Why are you giving me such a hard time? You're supposed
to be my girl." Lindsay was upset and getting angry.

Lindsay didn't want to, but I had to force her to deal
with the realities of having a child alone. "Exactly, I am
your girl, and my job is to tell you when you're making the
biggest mistake of your life!" I was upset too.

"Oh, I'm sorry. You're the expert. You can't even confront a man who sleeps in your bed night after night!" she
yelled back.

I leaned back to cool off. "Lindsay, what does Troy have
to say about all this?"

"I have everything—"

"I know, under control, like you always do!" I smarted.

"Listen, I don't want to talk about it anymore." Lindsay
was pissed.

"You can't keep running away from the truth, Lindsay."

"Try looking in the mirror, Charlie!" Lindsay said as she
walked to the door.

Chapter 37

Sobering Thoughts

To my unborn child . . . I pray today for you, and I ask not only that God forgive me, but that your spirit does too.

I waited until the last minute to go through with the abortion. The only comfort was Charlie being here with me.

"Charlie, I'm sorry about the things I said that day at the apartment."

"Girl, it's cool. When you're good friends, you're not out of line when you're telling the truth."

"You're getting good at this female bonding stuff."

"I know," Charlie said, rolling her eyes and smiling. "So, how are you holding up?" she asked.

"Tired, out of breath, and scared." I was reconsidering having my family help me raise the baby. But was that what I really wanted? To raise a child and be tied to Troy forever?

"What if I don't want to do it?" I asked.

"Surely you're not getting cold feet?"

"Look, I'm just worried. You know all this stuff in the media about career women and waiting too late to have kids. What if this is my only chance to have a baby and I blow it?"

"Lindsay, I'm not happy about being here either and believe me I feel your pain. I've been where you are."

We clasped hands tightly.

"I don't think you're ready for this. I've gotten to know you pretty well, and I know you're not ready for this yet. I also know you deserve someone who's gonna love *you* for *you*," Charlie said, trying not to sound preachy. "If I'm not ready, I'm not having it. Simple as that. But you have to do what's best for you. Raising a child is hard work, more than a notion, whether they are yours or not. Believe me. Every other weekend with Michael's kids was no picnic."

"I just want the best for my child. I want things to be perfect," I said.

"And they can be, Lindsay. Don't settle for being just another baby's mama. More importantly, don't settle for being eternally attached to an unworthy man."

Charlie made sense. I didn't want to punish a new life and bring it into a world that I hadn't conquered enough on my own.

As the anesthesia took effect, I closed my eyes and prayed it would all be over soon.

I woke up in a violent state, screaming, "No!" I balled up my fists as my body jerked forward. Bile disgorged from my mouth.

"It's just the anesthesia," the nurse informed Charlie. "She'll be fine."

Charlie was right there holding my hand.

My two-way pager went off. "Lindsay, your butt better be on the way to Ian Schrager's latest venture. The Hudson Hotel. Dinner in the Cafeteria. Drinks in the library, fireside." Judy always cluttered it with too much info. Unlike Tara's simple voicemail: "See you tonight. The Hudson. Fifty-eight and Ninth. Smooches."

Tara and Judy both had started questioning why I hadn't been hanging out as much lately. I wasn't intentionally trying to shun them, but I needed time to heal and get over Troy. I was also feeling like my friendship with them had come to an impasse.

I entered the library bar. The room was opulent, yet warm. Dark wood, the antique pool table, and large leather chairs evoked the character of a nineteenth-century social club. Tara and Judy lounged in front of a blazing fire. The panic of being a half hour late was all over my face. It had only been a week since the abortion and I still had to take it easy.

"Lindsay, I'm starving! You know I'm hypoglycemic. What took you so long?" Judy whined.

"I love you too," I said, ignoring her bitching.

"Enough already. Ladies, no cat fights," Tara said, briskly walking over to the main bar, leaving Judy and me bringing up the rear. She wanted to examine the Who's Who pit: a collection of people huddled around cocktail tables, some sat on Plexiglas stools, others in gilded Versace-like chairs. The eclectic design and fantastical murals made this place the hot ticket in town.

"Nobodies!" Tara casually remarked as we continued into the dining room.

The Hudson Cafeteria was quickly becoming my favorite chow spot. I loved the haute-comfort food. The open kitchen, with chefs tossing the contents of their skillets over raging flames, was a sight to watch. I especially loved the unpretentious communal seating arrangement.

"Did you guys see the cover of *Us* magazine? Lindsay, you remember your boy Shake? Well, I hear he's having another baby," Judy said. I almost gagged on my chicken. Thank God, I never told them about me and Shake.

"Yes, and Miss Thing already gets ten percent. That's what I'm talking about! Who cares if the man is around or not? It's about a check!" Tara said, stuffing her face with turkey meatloaf.

I'm *really* glad I kept my mouth shut.

"What kills me is that she is some gold-digging video dancer. I mean, why am I killing myself working so hard? I think we should stop trying to be high-powered bread-winning chicks. Let's be dumb, unambitious, and get the money!" Judy interjected. "What do you think, Lindsay?"

I wanted to stay away from the baby subject. "Oh, who cares about that stuff. Remember how much fun we used to have when we didn't have decent bank accounts," I said, abruptly changing the subject and giving the conversation an upbeat twist.

Tara and Judy looked at me as if I wasn't speaking English.

"What are you talking about, Lin Lin?"

"Come on, Tara, remember when your lights got cut off and we came over with candles," I said, "eating pizza and making our own music by singing our favorite songs. Tell me you don't miss our sleepovers?" I tried to take Tara and Judy with me, but they were not going there. "You can't buy good memories like ours."

"Well, I'll pay you to forget them," Judy said.

"I hope you don't go around telling others," Tara said. "That's what you do when you're broke and busted. We're not either of those anymore, so no more walks down memory lane, please." Tara was pissed. I felt like I was sitting with a total stranger.

I didn't know what to say next. I was lost. Here I was remembering our best times, times that I thought were the foundation of our friendship, and all Tara wanted to do was trash them. Something was happening to The Supremes—one of them wanted a solo act: me.

Chapter 38

Food for Thought

Charlie and I met at the corner of Sixth and Forty-second and proceeded into Bryant Park. Charlie handed me a brown paper bag. Lunch. The public library made the area peaceful and serene. Our search for a seat began.

The park was packed. An adult recess for the business people taking in a little fun in the sun. Men with their ties undone and sleeves rolled up; women in skirts and sneakers instead of high heels. A smile was on almost every face.

We lucked out when a couple left a bench facing a bright colorful rose garden free. The warmth of the bright sun blanketed our faces. We both smiled at our good fortune.

I quickly grew comfortable with my sack lunch of a turkey sandwich and chips and got an urge to blurt out what had been paining me since leaving dinner with Tara and Judy the night before.

"I think me and my buddies have moved in different directions."

Charlie stopped eating and shifted, taking her shoes off, crossing her legs Indian style.

"I've been feeling this way for a while, but I didn't want to deal with it."

"Lindsay, I think we've both been getting a heavy dose of reality lately."

"True," I continued. "The last time I was at dinner with Tara and Judy I kept seeing it. We weren't on the same wavelength at all. I couldn't even have a conversation of substance with them. I spent an entire evening with two women who were supposed to be my closest, *no*, my *best* friends, and I walked away feeling vacant."

"Lindsay, this doesn't mean you don't like them, you're just seeing that you're not them. Girl, life is about change."

A lightbulb went off in my brain, and I felt like dropping logic I'd been harboring for months, maybe years. "At this point, Charlie, it's beginning to feel very important that I associate with people who are trying to *do* something instead of just talking about wearing a two-hundred-dollar thingamajig and being invited to the best whatever."

"I hear you. It's about being intellectually and spiritually stimulated," Charlie agreed.

"Indeed it is!" I was reminded of the discussion I tuned

into after returning home from dinner. Tavis Smiley was moderating a panel discussion on TV about the state of black America. "Did you watch CNN last night?" Charlie was so overcome with enthusiasm she almost dropped her drink.

"Did I! I was hoping I wasn't the only one."

"Honey, thinking about dinner and listening to what all the politicians had to say made me dig deeper. But what's up with the state of black women in general?"

"Lindsay, we have so much potential, but not many of us have it all like you. Your boss might be crazy, but he's looking out for you."

"But I still have to fight. He isn't trying to give a woman his job."

"You got a point!" Charlie nodded in agreement. "For the most part, I think we just get frustrated. I know I do. We have to fight for so much that we get confused and start fighting each other. *Essence* did a big cover story on the same kind of thing. Black women and white women in the workplace."

"I know I read that!" I commented.

"It's funny, it made me open my eyes and rethink my entire view on Miranda and blond ambition. I'm sure they probably never grew up, went to school, or worked around anybody but white people. They honestly don't think we're qualified for the big executive jobs," Charlie said, getting excited.

"Well, you can't fix that without reversing four hundred years of oppression in our society," I sarcastically noted.

"Yeah, well, I'm going to do my best to make what we have to offer known. I'm going to stay on their asses to create more opportunities for other black women. Lindsay, history only repeats itself if you don't work for change."

"Absolutely, but you know 'we' black women can be hard on each other. So it's about rising above the negativity. I'm really going to go for it on my new show with Alix and push for black women to be hired behind the scenes too. And as far as Alix goes, I'm going to make sure her character continues to represent all sistas of the twenty-first century. God willing, I'm one black woman who is gonna open up some doors!"

"I've gotta represent in my scripts too. I want my female characters to be vulnerable *and* strong."

We were speaking truth on a meaningful subject.

"When it's all said and done, I think it's just that I've graduated. I can't do things the same way anymore. I don't want to be forty and talking about who's hot and who's not, waiting on Prince Charming to sweep me off my feet and take me shopping." I paused. "I know with Tara and Judy, there will always be a closeness between us, but they've got to understand that for me a lot of that b.s. we do is played out. I love them, but I can't keep sitting with yesterday."

"Maybe you've just moved in separate directions, or maybe somebody ain't moved nowhere," Charlie said, leaning back and taking a moment to do her own soul searching. "Girlfriend, you got me thinking now. I shut myself off too much to other sistas."

"Charlie, I agree. It wasn't so healthy how in the past you always hung by yourself, with Michael, or just with your gay friend, not that anything's wrong with that. But you've allowed yourself to be too narrow."

"I feel you. I want to broaden my vision too, Miss Lindsay."

We laughed.

"No, seriously we have to be more connected to each other." Charlie smiled and handed me a soda.

"It's about our making alliances with other women, and not just black, but white, Asian, Spanish, and Native American too. So you just make sure when that script of yours is finished, I get the first copy. I've got a girlfriend at Universal," I said.

"Make it happen, Lindsay!"

"Girlfriend has the juice to green-light projects too!"

We entertained ourselves for the rest of our lunch, plotting to make our own "girls' club," politics for the entire hour. Our friendship hit a new high.

"Charlie, we always chitchat, but today was like an archeological excavation of the mind," I said, finishing off my lunch.

"That's right, and our finds are the precious artifacts of knowledge, wisdom, and girl power!" Charlie smiled.

We exited the sanctuary of the park feeling as if we could save the world. We imagined all women, all sisters of color coming together, each feeling comfortable being who she was, instead of killing one another's spirits. After all, as a wise *man* once said, *Never underestimate the power of a woman.*

Chapter 39

Coffee...Ahh.
the Aroma

Rule Number 8: Throw that mental mess out with the rest of the garbage and start fresh!

I was packing up the last of my belongings, including my finished script. That's right, I finally finished it. After I returned from my engagement party in Buffalo, my writer's block disappeared. I came back and was a writing machine. I think Granny's magic words turned me around. Life is funny in another big way too. My friendship with Lindsay has helped me rediscover myself. But, out of all our wild and crazy missions, today was going to top them all. The "Old Charlie" was back in the game of life!

Fixing Charlie was the goal and, slowly but surely, I'm getting my act together. Loving God first and me second. I'm exercising three times a week—my body is definitely a temple—and I'm trying to write one to five pages a day on my next project: a science fiction screenplay. I will never put a man in front of my goals or happiness again.

Today is the day I leave Michael for good. I can't wait to see his face when he comes home tonight. It's a shame, he's been doing his thing with Natasha for so long, he's just comfortable and dumb. As of tonight, I won't be Brooklyn bound anymore. I'm *peacing* my mind on my new place and leaving the trouble behind in this sorry apartment where I've felt too much hurt.

The telephone interrupted my thoughts.

"Hello?" I said calmly.

"Hello. Is Michael there?"

It was Natasha. Was this perfect timing or what? Her voice made me laugh for some odd reason. Maybe it was that I finally had a better secret than she did.

"Natasha, Michael isn't here. I thought he was with you." She hadn't seen the side of Charlie I was about to give her. I was about to be bad and didn't care.

"I don't know what you're talking about. Why would he be with me? Look, we're just friends," she said.

"Oh, friends? I thought you all were business partners," I quizzed.

"Um, yes, that's what I meant, you see—"

"Natasha, shut up!" I cut right into her. "I know all about you and Michael. I also know your type. You're an old, sad, pitiful excuse for a woman, who preys on other women's men. One day you'll meet your match. Michael may not be smart enough to understand, but I damn sure am."

"I don't know what you're talking about. I told you, we are just friends." She was starting to choke up.

"First of all, bitch, don't interrupt me!" I heard her gasp. "Oh, it doesn't feel so good being called out of your name, does it?" Natasha was silent. "You're so used to calling here, hanging up, playing games, but this time I'm gonna finish! You can have Michael, no hard feelings. The best woman won. Me! His sorry ass is all yours!"

"I don't want Michael," she said with a shaky voice.

"Honey, tell me something I already don't know. Listen, I'll be gone in an hour, call back then."

I slammed the phone down as hard as I could. I was tired of Natasha's whiny, barely-speaking-English behind. I felt semi-victorious. Natasha wasn't the only unpleasant intrusion in my life. I had one more loose end to tie.

I picked up the phone, quickly punching in numbers.

"Juanita speaking. Holla at me." Baby Mama Drama herself picked up immediately.

"Hello, Juanita, this is Charlie. I've never called before now because I didn't have a reason to." I took a deep breath and continued, "Even though your children spoke badly to me, I never threw salt on your name."

"Ain't this a trip?" Juanita said venomously.

My nostrils flared. I didn't want to get into a shouting match but what I had to say was important. I had no choice but to lower myself to Juanita's level to make sure she understood. "I just wanted to give you a piece of advice. It's not a good idea to put your kids in adult business and have them fight your battles." My voice was tense.

"How you gonna call me and tell me what I can and cannot do with *my* kids?" Juanita said. I just knew she was on the other end rolling her eyes and neck.

"Clearly, somebody needs to tell you, you . . . " *Stupid!* I bit my lip, holding in the tail end of my thoughts. I started again slowly, "Juanita, you don't know me, or know what kind of woman I am. Do you realize the power I had with your kids?" I could tell that she was finally seeing where I was going. "Just think about all the stuff you've done to me. Think what I could have done to them, if I wanted to play the same dirty games you were playing. I could've been abusive, verbally or, even worse, physically abusive."

I could hear her exasperated breathing, but she was getting the message. "You dragged my name through the mud, and I could've done the same. There were so many times I could've made comparisons that I was prettier and smarter than you, I had a job but you were on welfare living in the projects, and that's why their daddy chose me." I went on and on spelling it out for Juanita. "To be quite honest, Juanita, I think I love your children more than you do. What other woman do you know would have taken all the mess you put me through, without some sort of retaliation? Are you still there?" I wanted to make sure she was still listening.

"Uh, yeah. I mean, yes, I'm still here." Juanita cleared her throat. It was obvious that she was paying close attention.

"I'm only telling you this because I'm leaving Michael. I really love MJ and Tiffany. I wanted to warn you. The next woman Michael gets with may not be a God-fearing woman like me." I wasn't sure, but based on the silence I think she was choked up. I knew she loved her kids, but somebody needed to show her that she's been wrong and that she's hurting her children's future.

"Well, that's all I wanted to say. Good luck."

"Charlie?" Juanita meekly said.

"Yes?"

"Um, thank you."

"You're welcome," I said as I hung up. That conversation with Juanita was a long time coming. I just hoped she would really remember what I passed on to her when the next woman in Michael's life rolled in.

I sat in the living room, scanning the empty apartment. Glad I settled up with Juanita and Natasha. This would all be a part of my past soon. But for some reason I still wasn't completely satisfied. I couldn't sit still. I had to move around the apartment. I couldn't believe how long I'd been Michael's fool.

It took me a long time to smell the coffee. Michael brewed it strong and hot, but I didn't want to have a cup of it, not even a sip! If this had been my mother instead of me, I would have judged her. Harshly.

The awful truth had me admitting just how judgmental I was. I had been looking down on my mother for years, when no matter what, she'd been there for me, through all of my ordeals, giving advice that I felt she was unqualified to give. Not once did my mother make me feel stupid or bad for staying with Michael. She loved me and would support whatever decision I made. She'd given me unconditional love, and now I wasn't so sure I deserved it.

I ran back into the living room, unpacked the telephone and plugged it into the wall. It was late, but not too late for my night-owl mother. After two rings Mama picked up.

"Hi, Mama. You know I love you. I tell you that every time I talk to you. But there's something I've never said, and need to say now." My voice quivered. So many emotions were surfacing.

"Charlie, is everything okay?" Mama was worried.

"Yes, everything is fine. I'm leaving Michael for good, but that's not why I called. Ma, I love you with all my heart. And more importantly, I *respect* you. I want and need you to know this. It's taken me a while to realize it. Also, it took some hard lessons in love and personal degradation to admit to myself that for years I've always looked down on you, and the choices you've made in life." The shame I felt caused me to cry.

"Baby, I know. I don't want you to feel guilty. I've made plenty of mistakes in my life. I'm just sorry you had to witness most of them." Mama started to cry too.

"But Ma, we all make mistakes. When I do, you never judge me. Please, forgive me?" I said, trying to wipe my face. My tears weren't for Michael, and I didn't want him coming in thinking they were.

"Stop crying, baby. There's nothing to forgive. We live and we learn. Don't think for one minute that I haven't learned a thing or two from you," she said, trying to sound hard-core. Her attempt lightened the moment. "But it feels real good to know that my baby girl respects me," Mama said, chuckling slightly.

"I do. I always have. It was always my problem not yours. I have to go. I just wanted to tell you how much I love and appreciate you." I needed to collect myself before Michael arrived.

"I know. Same here. Don't worry, you'll be fine, know that it's Michael who's lost." Mama blew me a kiss over the phone and hung up. Now I was ready to face my new life.

Michael entered the apartment, and when he hit the lights he was startled, but he tried to act unaffected. "Babe, what happened to the furniture?" Michael casually asked, looking around. The only thing still intact was that tired walk-in closet, and his clothes.

"Oh, I moved all my furniture to my new apartment. Remember, it was all mine. You can keep the place, like I said, I have a new one." I handed him my set of keys.

"Charlie, what the hell is going on?" Michael was pissed. Probably more so because he was going to have to cook and clean for himself now.

"You would know if you didn't have your head so far up Natasha's butt. By the way, she called earlier," I said with a smirk.

"Charlie, I know I was wrong, but I ended that months ago. I swear." Michael was sweating, and doing that fast talking again.

"You ended it? Oh, so now you're admitting something did happen." I shook my head.

"It didn't mean anything. I was just using her, baby. Please just listen to me, I can explain." Michael realized he was losing.

"When I first met you, I told you that I would be the coolest woman you would ever date. No nagging or questioning your whereabouts all the time. All I wanted from you was respect," I reminded Michael.

"I know, and you mean everything to me. Please Charlie, don't do this, I love you." Michael looked sorrowful.

"How can you love me, when you can't even respect me? You had that woman calling our house. Michael, calling *our* house." The way I looked and the harshness of my words let him know I wasn't his fool anymore.

"I hope Natasha was worth it. I pray she makes you and the kids very happy. And good luck on that new business." Granny gave me that last one, said the old folks used to say, "You get more flies with sugar than shit!" I was killing him with all the kindness in the world.

"Fuck! Charlie, please just wait! Just give me another chance!" Michael was starting to lose it. I picked up my small box of personal items and made my exit. I kept my head held high as I walked past Michael.

"It's gonna be hard, but I've got to move on with my life. I'll eventually get over you and I imagine you'll get over me. But what's more important is that I have to do what's right for me." I turned one last time before opening the door. "Why should I continue to press you to be faithful? A man who's true will be true. You feel me?" I said, looking Michael right in the eye. "Peace out, adiós, or better yet, as the *French* would say, au revoir!" I smarted off. I just couldn't help myself.

Michael would've married me. Just a little more time was all he needed, and my continued patience would be rewarded once I said, "I do." I still love Michael, but it's time for me to start loving myself. I'm finally doing what I feared most, starting over on my own. The fear of being alone was so powerful, but *now* my happiness feels just as strong.

I checked my watch, right on time. I walked out and headed across the street where Lindsay was pulling up in the getaway car. I'd risen out of Michael's destructive ashes like a phoenix!

Chapter 40

Mama's Eyes

"M" ama, I want to come home," my voice cracked. I didn't need to give an explanation or reason. Mama wanted me home too.

I was sitting at a small table in the back of Starbucks inside Lambert–St. Louis Airport waiting for Mama to pick me up. The airport was a drastic contrast from the Newark Airport bustle of businessmen and jet-setters.

A vision of timeless beauty, Mama appeared. She was dressed ethnic chic. Layers of scarves and Egyptian-print fabric draped her body. She jazzed up the ensemble with exaggerated beads around her neck and a hip pair of multicolored Prada sneakers, a present from me last Christmas. Mama's large gold bangles jingled softly as she held me tightly in her arms.

"So, how's my Lindsay?" Mama asked, emptying a tiny blue packet of sugar substitute into her coffee.

"I'm fine, Mama. I'm happy to see you." I doodled with the coffee stirrer.

"I want to talk before we go home."

There was a look in her eyes and I knew that a lesson was coming. Mama took a big swallow of the molten black liquid. "You need to come home more often. Family should be the most important thing in one's life."

Mama insisted I had gotten carried away with work and was too intense about life.

"Your family's gonna love you no matter what. Whether or not you have a job or know people in high places. You get so caught up in the little things, Lindsay. Things that add up to a bunch of nothing, like this whole relationship with Troy."

My sisters had opened their big mouths.

"Honey, please, your life is worth so much more than some little relationship. Stop worrying. When it's time, God will bring you the right one." Mama's words of wisdom stung. "How have you been feeling?" she said, examining me.

"I've been," I paused, "uhm, good."

"Humph, strangest thing, I dreamt about fishes. I was wondering if it was you." I shook my head no, but Mama knew, just like all mothers do when their babies aren't telling the truth. "I'm not happy about this abortion."

"Mama—" I tried to interrupt, but my mother shushed me.

"No, Lindsay, I love you too much to dance around all this. You're grown, but I birthed you. No more! Do I make myself clear?"

"Yes, Mama," I whispered softly.

"Life is nothing to play around with."

I was hoping Mama was done, but she wasn't.

"I meant what I said about that Troy stuff. I don't want another thought wasted on him. Do you read me?"

"Loud and clear!" I started to cry.

Mama wiped my face with a stiff napkin.

"Perfect example of what I mean when I say you waste too much time on the little things." She paused, then held my face in her hands. "Lindsay, your sister Faith needs us."

"What happened, Mama?" My heart skipped.

"The MS has gotten worse."

"What did the doctors say?" I asked.

"I don't know. But we're going to the hospital from here."

I sat still in the car. I couldn't stop crying. Multiple sclerosis was a cruel joke on the body. Thoughts of Faith's body shutting down, paralyzed to the point of being confined to a wheelchair, filled my head. I understood now more than ever that nothing is promised, and there are no guarantees in life.

The entire family was in the waiting room when Mama and I arrived. Daddy was so happy to see me he actually lifted me up in the air when we embraced. Daddy was normally a man of few words, but not today.

"I'm glad you're home, baby," he said, hugging me again.

I had been so distant my family didn't even expect me to show up, which reinforced what had become clear to me—that I was definitely going down the wrong path. My nieces and nephews greeted me with innocent and tentative affection. My brother-in-law Richard's face was emotionless. He had to be strong for the kids, but his bear hug told me just how much he was hurting.

Holding two cups of coffee, Angie entered the waiting room. She wasn't her usual big-mouthed, brassy self. Today she was weary and softspoken. She looked at me as if she had seen a ghost. I had to be the strong one for a change. We hugged and held each other tight for several minutes.

"I'm sorry I've been such a jerk," I said.

"It's okay. Little sisters are usually jerks," Angie joked, "but I still love you."

Faith was diagnosed primary-progressive. Angie and I stood, one on either side of her bed, each holding one of her hands. Faith was trying hard to speak.

"Finally, a way to shut you up," Angie said.

"I guess Dr. Chang's magic tea didn't work too well, and neither did the good folks at Hannah's Herbal. Man, I'm zero for two with you," I joked.

Faith's laughter triggered a domino effect. We all started laughing and crying all at the same time. Faith had to make us stop because laughing hurt.

"Look what I have to do, just to see you," Faith said sarcastically.

"Yeah, well my facial was canceled, and I had nothing else to do," I joked.

Faith lay helpless. Angie got quiet. She always clammed up when she was nervous or scared, sometimes she just burst into tears, and she was on the verge.

I couldn't believe how selfish I'd been all this time. My sisters had taken my side in all my complaining and bitching about Robert and held on for dear life through all my relationship roller-coaster rides. Not once had I even asked, *How's your life? Or, How was your day?*

I was trying my best not to break down as I slowly ran a brush through Faith's thick and wavy hair. Faith motioned for Angie to sit down.

"I remember when you were a little girl and me and Angie used to brush your hair. Funny, huh?" Faith paused. "Angie and Lindsay, I trust you with everything I own, including my babies. I want you to make sure they're taken care of if something happens to me."

I stopped brushing. I didn't want her talking like she had been given a death sentence. Angie stood up and grabbed my hand, placing it between hers and Faith's. Faith wanted both of us to understand that her quality of life was going to change now because of her sickness. The room had become too morbid for me. I quickly changed the subject.

"Guess what y'all? I finally stood up to Robert, and I'm gonna start relaxing more and making time for myself and my family," I said, trying to hide my fear.

"Good, I'm so proud of you, and I'm going to ask God to bring you a good man," Faith replied with a weak smile.

I was blown away by Faith's selflessness. Faith was sick, laid up in the hospital, but still praying for us. I touched Faith's face. Being with my sisters made me really understand the importance of living each day like it's your last. With all of life's uncertainties, the *only* guarantee is family.

Chapter 41

Emancipation Night

I sashayed into the Shark Bar glowing, hidden behind a large crystal vase of roses with a huge smile on my face. I was about to shock the socks off Charlie with my new look. A chopped-off layered bob. Maria had had a fiesta on my head as she cut, snipped, and teased my once bland and basic do. I was a new woman draped in a lavender pashmina.

"Would you look at what the cat dragged in," Charlie said, twirling in her chair.

"I like to be fashionably late."

Charlie pulled out the barstool and relieved me of the flowers.

"Oh no, you didn't!" she screeched at the sight of my hair.

"I needed a change."

Charlie was awestruck and Stevie stood lockjawed.

"There you go. Now you know only white girls pull some mess like this. Cutting their hair off when they need a change."

"But that hair is hot, *Mami*!" Stevie flirtatiously gave his two cents.

"Okay, okay. I'll give it to you. The hair is fly." Charlie raised her glass.

My metamorphosis was complete. I'd truly gone and gotten a new attitude. Stevie busied himself so Charlie and I could catch up.

"That time off with your family did you a world of good. You look great."

"It was an eye opener."

"How's your sister Faith?"

"She's making it. I'm gonna go check her out again next weekend. The doctor's started her on steroids, but I hope they don't keep her on those long. She's a fighter. In the meantime, it's in God's hands."

"I'll keep her in my prayers," Charlie said, trying to peek at the card attached to the flowers. "And the flowers—"

"A thoughtful gesture from Robert! He was really concerned about my family too."

Stevie grabbed a nearby martini glass and tapped a knife lightly against its rim.

"To Charlie's first script being completed, a welcome

back to Lindsay and her rocking new look, and a speedy recovery to her sister."

Charlie interrupted. "I've got an announcement. I guess I was being a little too hard on Miranda. I thought she was giving me the runaround, but we finally sat down and it turns out she'd been working things out with HR all this time."

"HR?" I said.

"Yep, to make sure my bonus check was substantial." Charlie whipped out her bonus check. "*Pladow!* To getting my drinking partner back! Drinks on me!"

My cell interrupted. Stevie knew the drill. He reached to turn down the music.

"Don't you dare, Stevie." I casually answered, "Hello?"

"Lindsay, it's Robert. I know it's your personal time, but I'm just calling to make sure your first day back was a good one."

"As a matter of fact, it was a great one!"

"I'm glad to hear that." Robert gave a thoughtful pause. "By the way, do you or your family need anything?"

"No, but thanks, and the flowers are beautiful."

"Oh and FYI, I decided to get rid of Mark Peters. You figure it out."

"Are you saying?"

"Come on, Lindsay, what's my biggest peeve? If you know the answer to something, don't ask a stupid question."

"Robert, don't go there." My voice tightened up.

"I'm joking. Where's that great Lindsay sense of humor?" Robert chuckled.

"I'm sorry I snapped at you."

"Look, Lindsay, I just want you to be sharp, be the best."

"Robert, you think I don't want to be the best?"

"I know you do, and you will be. One last thing . . . I think you're ready."

I gave Charlie and Stevie the thumbs up.

"No, Robert, I know I'm ready!"

I gleefully hung up and spun around on my stool. Stevie snapped two rosebuds loose, placing one in my hair, then the other in Charlie's.

"Tonight, we dance!" he declared.

A small group of people leaving the restaurant made their way from the back. Troy stood squarely in the middle. He spotted me right away, and rushed over like we were buddies.

"Lindsay, I thought that was you."

"Yes, it's me. How are you, Troy?" My face was expressionless as I emphasized his name.

Stevie and Charlie stood close like guards. Troy felt their cold stares and leaned into me.

"Can I have a moment with you?"

I calmly nodded, reached for my drink, and led Troy to a neutral area a few feet away from the bar. My body language told him he was on my territory.

"I hope she doesn't give in to him. Look at him, the devil himself," Stevie said to Charlie.

"She won't. I'll kill her if she does."

I couldn't freak and give in to him. I had to face my fear.

"How've you been?"

"Good, actually great," I abruptly replied.

In an instant all the crap I'd gone through, right up to

the moment the anesthesia took me out, flashed before my eyes. Just thinking about it made me furious. Troy leaned back, sensing my anger. He tilted his head and I was caught mid-blink. Troy looked me up and down, inside and out. "You look great, Lindsay, and I really like your new hairstyle." Troy began to seduce me with those eyes of his. He was penetrating my mind speaking his syrupy sweet bullshit.

"Baby, I'm sorry things ended so nastily with us."

I started to crumble. I took the last sip of my Cosmo, searching for a way back. Troy motioned to Stevie, who growled under his breath, bucking up. Troy was confident, pointing to my empty glass.

"How about it?"

"Actually, no. Thanks, I've had enough."

I was doing my best to hold it together. Resisting his offer was smart, but I was still stuck on his eyes. He tried to stroke my hair, but I jumped back. The spell was broken. He had invaded too much of my personal space. Then Troy did the ultimate. He laughed, just like he did the day I told him about the baby. He laughed real good and said, "Yo, was that stuff about being pregnant true?"

"What!" The disgust on my face showed exactly what I was thinking, *There is no end to this loser's audacity.*

"It's just I thought you were lying." Troy had crossed the line for the last time.

A boost of strength surged through me and I was ready to knock him out, but something else happened. I was reminded, *"You may not change the world, but you can maintain your own dignity and integrity."* That damn book was haunting me with another lecture. I shook it off, but inside my body a showdown between good and evil had erupted. Voices in my head were screaming back and forth, *Go for it! Do it!* Then, *No! Don't play yourself girl!* In an instant I grew up, just like that. I decided to go out with class. I faced my demons like a woman.

"Are you out of your mind thinkin' you could have that much nerve saying something so cruel to me? Have you no shame? It was your child too!"

I didn't give Troy a chance to utter a word. I wanted to be adult, but I was no punk.

"You are one sick man. The old Lindsay would be tearing you a new one right about now, but you're not worth it," I said, without raising my voice, but Troy could feel my anger and my power. "One day you're gonna get all you deserve and more, and when karma strikes . . . I feel sorry for anybody with you. So take your lies and get out of my face! Consider yourself lucky. I'm too damn busy to be bothered."

I turned my back and proceeded to walk toward Charlie and Stevie. The next thing I knew, Troy was putting his hands on me. He grabbed me by the arm, trying to force me to face him.

"Don't you ever turn your back on me!"

My heart raced. "Negro, you must be crazy. My own father never put his hands on me."

Stevie must have overheard me, because like a flash of lightning, he hopped over the bar and snatched Troy up by the collar. All I saw were feet dangling and swinging in the air. I brushed myself off. By that time Charlie had rushed over, and damn near tried to kill Troy. Charlie grabbed everything that was movable—ashtrays, glasses, forks, even napkins. Stevie threw Troy out.

The patrons in the Shark Bar dispersed. Various looks of amazement were glued to their faces. Stevie and Charlie had saved the day, and some people started to clap. Stevie called out, "Show's over, people."

He put his arms around Charlie and me, making sure we were safe.

"Thank you, Stevie, for saving the day," I said humbly.

"Like Superman!" Charlie said, cracking up.

We were laughing so hard tears were pouring from our eyes.

"I guess I did good, huh?" I said, between the chuckles.

"You did great!" Charlie cheered.

"I'm finally over him. Turning the other cheek is new for me. Redemption is a good thing."

"Retribution is better! I'm proud of you, girlfriend," Charlie said.

I grabbed a nearby barstool and jumped on top of it.

"What are you doing, fool?" Charlie said, trying to pull me down.

"Hold on. I have a pact we need to sign off on."

"Let's hear it."

"It's our *new* mission. From now on we both have to promise to put ourselves first," I announced.

"Hear! Hear! No more sacrificing and settling when it comes to our happiness."

"And, when it comes to a man, it's give and take! Love is a two-way street."

"It's all about us from now on!"

"To being fierce, fabulous, and fearless!" I said, ending my speech.

"All right!" Charlie said, helping me down. We sealed our pact with a hug.

"Enough of all this sentimental stuff. Let's get this party started!" Stevie said with a sly grin.

"Let's do this!" I said.

"It's Friday and we just got paid," Charlie sang as she flashed a twenty and placed it on the bar.

The Shark Bar was closing, but the night was young. Stevie pushed two freshly filled glasses toward us.

"New one tonight, raspberry. This one's on me."

"Thanks!" We gladly accepted. We were more than willing to be his guinea pigs.

Stevie placed both elbows down on the bar and positioned himself directly in the middle of us.

"You know I've seen and learned a lot just by listening to you ladies, especially after what happened tonight. I know exactly what you've been going through. I've been dying to put my two cents in 'cause, girlfriends, men are definitely a trip!" Stevie chirped in a high-pitched tone.

Charlie and I both stood perplexed, mouths agape. He gave us a look as if to say we'd better not choke. Then he hit the stereo volume as "Lady Marmalade" pumped in. Charlie and I shrugged our shoulders. Stevie gave two snaps.

"Hello, don't get brand new on me. Getting all shy now."

All our fantasies of screwing him blind went up in smoke. Stevie *literally* "came out" from behind the bar. He grabbed Charlie's hand and they started dancing. Then Charlie started chanting.

"Scan-dal, scan-dal!" Charlie shoved a drink in my hand,

and began to dance around Stevie, and I was sputtering, trying to figure out how I never noticed.

"How could he deny the female race with *all that* body?" I asked.

"Chill out! You're overanalyzing things. Just get over it, there will be others. Plus we can still pretend and dream about Stevie being our boy toy."

I gave up and joined in, and we all chanted.

"Scan-dal, scan-dal!"

It was going to be a long night. Stevie danced back over to the bar and began setting up more Cosmos.

"Sorry, girl, I never did find that killer dress," I said.

"I guess it was a sign," Charlie said, patting me on the shoulder. "By the way, I still have the ring, but I was thinking about giving it back!"

"Fool! Do you know what kind of pendant two and a half carats could make?"

I shook my head. It was going to be a *very* long night.

Epilogue

Lindsay Has Her Say

That night at the Shark Bar was a triumph. Charlie and I were soldiers who had gone off to battle and returned home safely, despite the many casualties along the way. Many times our talks ran deep into the night and renewed a sense of self and self-worth in both of us. Charlie and I learned in the end to let go and live, and that this love thing is about survival of the fittest.

Meeting Charlie sent a resounding revelation through my brain. I was late learning, *but* I learned, women have the power to heal each other through friendship. We were two women from two different backgrounds, but that didn't matter. Our lives were a lot more similar than one would immediately suspect. I was the hopeless romantic, driven by career. Charlie was the kind of woman who knew better than to wear her heart on her sleeve.

So this meeting by chance, coincidence, fate, or whatever you want to call it, started something really special and wonderful. The close bond Charlie and I developed became both therapeutic and sinfully fun. Two little girls from small towns set off to the "Big City" to make good.

Both of us took a long time and went through a lot of drama to get to a good place in our lives with men, a place of peace. I was still so amazed by how in control Charlie seemed when it came to Michael, right up to the end. However, she admitted letting her guard down with him. Even the most controlled of us loses control every now and then.

In the end, it doesn't matter how confident or secure a woman is, she may still have some hidden insecurities. The key is to never stop working on them, because everyone's given a little bit of time here on this earth and there's no sense walking around hurt, bitter, and sad because a relationship didn't go your way. It's okay to be selfish, because if you're not happy, you can't make anybody else happy. And to hell with potential, a woman can't operate on the "mights" or "maybes," only on what is.

My best advice is that if something feels disjointed or bad, then take heed and move on. The worst thing a woman can do is give a man the satisfaction of seeing her all crumpled up.

But remember, it's okay to cry. Crying is cleansing.

Don't be afraid to cry till your eyes won't cry anymore. But after the tears, rebuild yourself. Focus on your job, your faith, work out, get a hobby—something. Just separate yourself from all the pain. Remember, success is the best revenge. Wish that man well and keep rollin'.

Charlie and I are still learning and growing, and have a whole lot more to experience with men. We know we're gonna make a few mistakes, but at the end of the day, we have each other's backs.

Cosmopolitan Girls' Advice

The kind only a true friend will give...

1. Show Off Your Fly-Girl Style. Pull out those tight jeans, that micromini, or clingy dress. Anything that makes you feel sexy. Put it on, prance down to the nearest dance floor, and shake what your mama gave ya!

2. Discover Your Beauty. Never let a man break your spirit and bring you to the point of insecurity and self-pity. Don't forget how beautiful and smart you are. Now repeat: Mirror, mirror on the wall, I *am* the most fabulous of them all!

3. It's Not Her Fault. Learn *not* to take your anger, frustration, and hurt out on the woman your man's dating now.

Let it go! If the other woman has some dirt on her hands, it all comes out in the wash eventually. What goes around comes around. Trust that!

4. Who's Trickin' Whom? All these designer shoes from Gucci to Manolo Blahnik, clothes, furs, iced-out Rolex, and fancy cars . . . Yes, you look good, but where's your self-worth? What you're getting has a price but what he's getting is priceless! Think about it. Who's tricking whom?!

5. Three Key Acts to Beware Of. (1) Drive-bys and Stake-outs: Driving by your ex-man's house in the wee hours, checking on the activity inside and for signs that he's not alone. Once you've done your drive-by, you may not be convinced enough. So you *park* your car and wait until you see movement. **(2) Bum's Rushes:** You see your ex out with a new woman and become so enraged that you rush the brotha and have to be physically held back by your girl-friend. **(3) DWI:** Dialing While Intoxicated—You've been out partying with friends, get wasted, and proceed to whip out your cell to call your ex, and end up making a fool of yourself. **Note:** If you feel any one of these three symptoms coming on, please run to your nearest friend and tell her to STOP you.

6. Smell the Coffee. This is an easy one. If you're more committed to the relationship mentally, physically, and fi-nancially, wake up and smell the coffee!

7. Sex Is Trendy, Life Isn't. No condoms, no way! Which is more important, "Ooh, ooh, baby!" or "Oh, shit!" And did I forget to mention herpes, HIV, AIDS, or a host of other venereal diseases? The choice is yours. Be smart!

8. Don't Play Yourself. If he hasn't returned your calls, e-mails, or letters, don't press or stress yourself, him, or your friends. It's time to step! Remember: watch what he does, not what he says.

9. Get Your Own. If you can only reach him by cell or pager, have never been to his house, he has to call you, and he never takes you out on dates in public places, then you can be almost 100 percent sure that he has a wife, wifey, woman, or girlfriend. Chile, you know you're wrong.

10. Have Courage. Ask God for the strength and wisdom to get out of a bad situation. Then get a hobby, exercise, read a book, do whatever to get on with your life. And don't you dare carry that old baggage with you into the new life that awaits you.

11. Take a Self Day. Make time for the "queen"—*you!* Get that hair done, those nail and toes done, and treat yourself to an expensive meal. Looking like a million bucks comes in handy, too, when you run into your ex.

12. Do the 3 D's. Simply do something "daring and deliciously drastic." Nothing more and nothing less! Maybe even throw the bomb-ass party for yourself while you're at it. Invite everyone you know. You'll be the talk of the town!

Feel free to copy these pages and carry them with you. In case of emergency, just reread them. . . . for strength and inspiration.

Cosmopolitan Girls' Acknowledgments

Very Special Thanks to our agent extraordinaire, Marie Dutton Brown, for your guidance, and helping to shape and breathe life into *Cosmopolitan Girls*.

Extra Special Thanks to Janet Hill, our friend and editor. You truly understood the lifestyle, the realities and fantasies, the happiness and heartaches of today's "Cosmopolitan Girls." Again, thank you for your unparalleled vision and commitment.

Special Thanks to Calvin Chu for a wonderful cover.

This book would not have been a reality without the tireless support and effort from the following individuals and organizations: Alan Haymon; Tavis Smiley; Tynisha Thompson and Khalid Williams of Marie Brown Associates; Laini Brown; Patrik Henry Bass of *Essence* magazine for your enthusiasm and early support; Sherry Bronfman; Patti Webster; Karen Lee; Norma Augenblick; Keith Clinkscales and Leonard Burnett of Vanguarde Media; Mc-Clean Greaves, Dan Ivy, Peter Baker, and the fantastic staff at the Hudson Hotel; the gracious staff of LaSamana for comfort and peace; Two Bunch Palms; Saundra Parks of the Daily Blossom; Jeffrey Scales; Emmett Dennis of Blue Flame Marketing; Ira Jones of First Civilization; Jabari

Asim; Jamale Ridgway; and Emily Bosco of Absolut, our honorary Cosmo Girl, for all your support.

Lyah Beth LeFlore's Acknowledgments

Marie Dutton Brown, thank you for your advice, knowledge, dedication, and unflagging support. Here's to many more fruitful endeavors.

Tavis Smiley, you are truly a class act and a dear friend. Thank you for your early support and insight.

Family: my big brother, John Drew Lindsay; my Aunt Cynthia LeFlore; Francis Crawford; the LeFlores; the Davis-Bradley descendants; the Bohrs; the Lemmons; the Jarmon decendants of Decatur, Illinois; the Jenkins-Robnett families; the Price-Moore families; the Lindsays.

Extended family: Rudolph Nickens, Billy Crumpton, Billie Jean and Earl Wilson, Charles Wartts, Curtis Lyle, Bruce Purse, JD Parran, the Lakes, Margurite Hightower, Aunt Shirley Bedford and members of the Semper Fidelis Social Club, Marsha Caan, Vola Washington.

My cousin-girlfriends: Karen Bohr, Passion Bragg, Africa Lake, ShaRee Meyers, Gigi Hill, Sydney Thornton, Susan Garrett, Tracey Mack, Kim Mosby.

My other big sisters: Lesvia Castro, Crystal Gore, Delphine Pruitt, Sable Jones, Kathy Bedford, Teresa Anderson, Daphne Moore.

To my girls with whom I share many wonderful memories: Constance Orlando, for opening your home to me and cheering me on through the final stretch; Dana Hill, Leslie Williams, Mary Crockett-Smith, Lajuan Murphy-Williams,

Keita Turner, Crystal Frazier, Sandra Hernandez, Monifa Carter, Leah Moskowitz, Dion Peroneau, Takia "Tizzi" Green, the Ladies of Alpha Kappa Alpha Sorority, Inc., and especially the undergraduate sorors of Delta Tau Chapter 1988–1991.

It's equally important for women to have great male friends: Scott Crawford, Charles Berry, Alan Bovinett, and Damu Mtume. Chivalry is *not* dead!

To the special men in my life with style who make me look and feel glamorous: Richard Owings, Aaron Mitchell, Edwin Pabon, Wilfredo Rosado of Edmundo Castillo, and Quentin Harris.

To Jeffrey Scales, an incredible artist and photographer.

To my former employers: Herb Scannell, Andre Harrell, and Dick Wolf for recognizing my talents early on in my career.

Charlotte Burley's Acknowledgments

A HUGE THANKS to my parents, Janice and Lamont Burley, for exposing me at an early age to everything life has to offer—the good times, hard times, and desperate times—allowing me to see for myself the many roads I could travel. Most importantly for allowing me to pick my own road. I love you so much for that!

Thanks to my brother Lamont Burley Jr., a.k.a. lil'man, and his wife Kelly for giving me precious gifts I'm proud to call nephews, I love you all! I also want to thank you for protecting me, my rights, and my freedom on a daily basis as Specialist Burley in the Army. I'm very proud of you!

Rhonda and Ronnie Jr. Frida, my cousins. This book is in your loving memory. You are truly loved and missed!

A special thanks to my grandparents George and Mary Baxter and my Aunt Linda and Uncle Ronnie Frida. Because of you I know that "true love" does exist.

Granny, you inspire me to never give up, you were living proof that you can achieve your dream!

Thanks to Beverly and Marcus Burley and Michael Young, evidence that not all stepmothers and stepbrothers are wicked. Love you guys.

To my best friends (a.k.a. lifers) who never ever said, "Stop dreaming." Thanks so much for being a POSITIVE in my life! Lee-Lee Walker, Kenny Headley, and Mclean Greaves, I love you dearly!

To my Jewish family: the Freilichs' Aaron, Sara, Michael, Ruthie, and Natalie, thanks for making NYC my second home. Love you guys!

To Danny Harris, my first love. I will always treasure the time we did have on this earth. May your soul rest in peace.

To my Sci Fi Family, thanks for your love and support. Very special thanks to Danny Ivy, Tony Reid, William Stewart, Javier Perea, and Will Wigley. You're always there when I need you, love you!

To my friend and photographer Jennifer Kilberg, thanks for making me look like a star, your talent amazes me.

To my other mother, friend, and agent Marie Dutton Brown, thank you for believing in me, scolding me, and loving me. When I grow up, I want to be just like you! Love you!

Cosmopolitan Girls:
A Reading Guide

About This Reading Guide

Lindsay Bradley and Charlie Thornton are the quintessential women of the new millennium—smart, sexy, spiritual, flawed, determined, and relentless. Whether they are on a quest to fulfill the Cosmo Girl Code of Arms or weathering the unpredictable turns in their love and professional lives, Lindsay and Charlie prove that women have the power to heal each other. We hope that your reading group finds inspiration in their story. The questions that follow are designed to spark a discussion that is poignant, hilarious, compelling, and deliciously intoxicating—as Lindsay and Charlie would like. So, girlfriends, put on your favorite big T-shirt, grab a Cosmo and some Kleenex, and get comfortable. Guys, pay close attention, feel free to chime in, and, well, take notes.

Discussion Questions

1. Lindsay appears to have it all together with a great job and a fabulous social life. Why is she so strong and together when it comes to taking care of business, but allows her emotions to take her off her game?

2. During Charlie's "pity party" at the beginning of the book, she says she "tossed her goals to the side and put other people's happiness first." What happens when you toss your goals to the side?

3. In "Prince Charming," Lindsay and Robert share an awkward moment where they connect before Troy enters. What if Troy hadn't interrupted; do you think Lindsay would have pursued Robert's subtle invitation? What do you think the implications would have been if she'd gotten involved with her boss? In examining corporate America, is there a double standard when it comes to women dating in the workplace?

4. When Lindsay and Charlie meet, it's the classic case of each one thinking the other's grass is greener. However, they discover they are two sides of the same coin. How do they reveal their similarities and differences?

5. Lindsay is flooded with opinions and advice from her sisters, her "girls" Tara and Judy, and her newfound friend Charlie. Discuss their differences of opinions. Do you think Lindsay deserved a second chance?

6. Lindsay and Charlie devise the Cosmo Code of Arms, proving that strength is in numbers, and becoming hell-bent on getting "payback." However, their vengeful tactics, disguised as fun-filled missions, lead to unexpected consequences. What are those consequences? When is enough enough? Do you recall if you or a friend has ever allowed such a situation to go too far in a relationship?

7. Charlie's own problems cause her to encourage Lindsay not to go down without a good fight after Troy breaks up with her. Why doesn't she have the same fighting spirit when it comes to dealing with Michael?

8. Discuss Charlie's attitude toward friendships with other women prior to meeting Lindsay. Do you know any women who have shut themselves off to friendships with other women?

9. Spirituality plays a big part in Lindsay and Charlie's lives. Recount and discuss the chapters that reveal various eye-opening moments in the story for both Lindsay and Charlie—moments that ultimately lead each woman to rediscover and renew her own spirituality and step out on faith. How important is *your* spirituality in your personal and professional life?

10. Charlie has a penchant for being judgmental when it comes to her mother, whom she describes as a "doormat for men." Her motto is "A man has never and will never define me." What does it take for women to wake up and smell the coffee?

11. Lindsay plays into Robert's philosophy that "one should avoid excessive socializing." She never mixes the business Lindsay with the social Lindsay. Why is she intimidated by his calls? How do you balance your professional life with your social life?

12. Charlie refers to the sacrifices she's made in order to make her relationship with Michael work. She says it was a "price she was willing to pay." Were all these sacrifices worth saving the relationship? Have you ever had friends who dated a man with children from a previous relationship? Did they encounter or experience the strain of "baby mama drama"?

13. Charlie's self-inflicted writer's block and her denial about her crumbling relationship with Michael have caused her to give up on her dreams, and she's fallen into a "safe rut." How does this happen, and why?

14. What does Lindsay mean when she describes the feeling she had after dinner with Tara and Judy as "vacant"? Do you have people in your life who are "sitting with yesterday"?

15. New York City is sexy, electric, and the center of the fashion, cultural, and social universes. Explore and discuss the "Big Apple" as the backdrop for the story, and how it becomes a character itself. What is its significance in Lindsay and Charlie's lives? In their friendship?

16. In "Food for Thought," Charlie raises the point that women "have to fight so much that we get confused and

start fighting each other." Do you agree or disagree? Lindsay also proclaims that women have to "stop killing each other's spirits." What does this mean to you? Discuss creating a "girls' club" of your own. What would you do? Finally, Lindsay describes her and Charlie's heart-to-heart as an "excavation of the minds." Create your own archaeological excavation of the minds within your group, and discuss women developing mutual-support systems and working together.

17. In "Emancipation Night," Lindsay and Charlie's new mission is to put themselves first and never compromise on their happiness. Discuss the growing pains both women endured. What does it mean to be fierce, fabulous, and fearless?

18. The birth of the Cosmo Code of Arms gives Lindsay and Charlie a marvelous new manifesto. Devise and discuss your own Cosmo Code of Arms.

About the Authors

Charlotte Burley was born and raised in Buffalo, New York. Burley moved to New York City and met computer genius Mclean Greaves. They teamed up to form Virtual Melanin, Inc. (VMI), a critically acclaimed Internet company specializing in urban content. VMI has earned rave reviews from *The New Yorker*, the *New York Times*, and the *Village Voice*. In 2001, Burley became a writer producer for the Sci Fi Channel. In December 2002 she created an image campaign entitled "Tattoo Man." It was used as the signature for the new look of Sci Fi. The spot garnered critical acclaim and won the 2003 Bronze CLIO Award, the AICP Award, London's 2003 AD&D Award, and three

2003 Promax/BDA Awards. Finally, as a result of the hugely successful "Tattoo Man" on-air campaign, the Sci Fi Channel became the first television network to be added to the Museum of Modern Art's (MOMA) historical art collection. Her future plans are with Tri-Media. She's excited to see what fresh and innovative writing she can conjure up in the near future.

Lyah Beth LeFlore, vice president of production and development for Alan Haymon Entertainment, Inc. (AHE), is making a name for herself in the world of television at the age of thirty-three. In 1995, LeFlore was profiled in *Essence* magazine's 25th Anniversary issue in the article "25 to Watch Under 25." LeFlore was born and raised in St. Louis, Missouri, and graduated from Stephens College with intentions of becoming a news reporter. However, after writing a TV segment on music artist MC Hammer for WAVE-3, the Louisville, Kentucky, NBC affiliate, during a fellowship through the National Association for Black Journalists (NABJ), she discovered her true talent and interest: television production. Since that time she has worked as a consultant on HBO's *Midnight Mac*, as development executive for FOX's *Between Brothers* and *Lawless*, as associate producer for FOX's *New York Undercover*, and as producer for the UPN shows *Grown Ups* and *Off Limits*. LeFlore is currently in development on several television projects, including the Disney Channel's animated series *Arooma Zoom Zoom*.